McFLANNELS UNITED

McFLANNELS
UNITED

HELEN W. PRYDE

THOMAS NELSON AND SONS LTD
LONDON EDINBURGH PARIS MELBOURNE
TORONTO AND NEW YORK

THOMAS NELSON AND SONS LTD

Parkside Works Edinburgh 9
3 Henrietta Street London WC2
312 Flinders Street Melbourne C1

THOMAS NELSON AND SONS (CANADA) LTD
91–93 Wellington Street West   Toronto 1

THOMAS NELSON AND SONS
385 Madison Avenue New York 17

SOCIÉTÉ FRANÇAISE D'EDITIONS NELSON
25 rue Henri Barbusse Paris Vᵉ

———

First published 1949

CONTENTS

TO
GLADYS

CHAPTER I

COUNTRY COUSIN

THE war was over. Matt McFlannel was safe. For his mother there need be no more sleepless nights during which she would torture herself with visions of torpedoes and broken ships and men ; instead there was the joy of wakening in the mornings and calculating that it was now one day nearer the sailor's homecoming. But Matt, doing the unexpected as was his wont, decided to remain at sea for a bit. This decision rankled in his mother's mind, and for days she brooded over what she felt was an insult to his home and family.

The sailor's father, his brother Peter and his sister Maisie all suffered under the cloud of Mrs McFlannel's complaints, but a ray of relief shone for them on the day on which a letter arrived from Sarah's half-forgotten sister Bella. The bewildered recipient read it aloud to her family :

> Dear Sarah, you will be surprised to see from the address that we are now living in Drumforber. Our oldest girl Sheena is coming to Glasgow to see about a job in connection with one of the hospitals. She is to see the matron at nine o'clock on Monday morning, and as there isn't a train from here on Sundays I wondered if you could put her up for the week-end. She won't be any trouble. I am sorry to be giving you such short notice but she only heard about this job yesterday. She will be arriving in Glasgow about seven o'clock on Saturday night. . . .

Sarah stopped reading to gape at her audience. ' My goodness ! ' she exclaimed. ' That's tonight ! She's got a nerve, so she

I

has ! Not to send me a scrape of the pen for about ten years and now this ! '

' Is there more to come ? ' asked Maisie.

Sarah read on :

I have a few hens, so I will send some eggs with Sheena. . . .

' Jeengs,' observed her husband. ' Fur some eggs Ah'd pit up wi' a dozen Sheenies.'

' Sheena, Dad. Not Sheenie.' The correction came, as was to be expected, from Maisie-the-teacher. ' Go on, Mother.'

If one of you could meet her at Buchanan Street station she'll be wearing an oatmeal coat and a red hat. . . .

' And,' queried Peter, with adolescent mirth at his own wit, ' if none of us meet her, will she be wearing nothing at all ? '

True to form, Sarah told him not to be vulgar, before resuming her reading :

The weather is very cold just now. Your loving sister Bella. PS Kind regards to all.

' Well, I like that ! ' stormed Sarah. ' As cool as a cucumber —after all these years ! '

Said Maisie : ' There's no time to lose, Mother. We'd better get Matt's room ready.'

' No, it might be damp after being empty so long. She'd better sleep with you, Maisie.'

' Ah tell ye whit,' put in Willie. ' You can sleep wi' Maisie, Serah, an' Ah'll sleep in the room bed alang wi' Peter. That'll leave the kitchen bed here fur the lassie.'

Sarah snorted. ' The very idea ! Putting a visitor in the kitchen bed ! '

' Ah think it's a grand idea ! ' was her husband's retort. ' Efter a', if she's comin' f'ae a wee place like whit-ye-may-ca'-it, she'll be used wi' sleepin' in waur places nor a kitchen bed.'

As Maisie went to search the gazetteer for the exact situation of Drumforber, Peter asked who was to meet the girl at the station.

'I think you'd better go yourself,' said his mother.

'No fear ! I'd hate any of the chaps in the works to see me along with this country cousin. She'll be some guy, all right, if her coat's made from oatmeal.'

'Don't be silly !' snapped Maisie from the bookcase. 'It'll be the colour of oatmeal.'

'If you're as wise as all that,' snapped back Peter, 'you'd be better to meet her yourself and help to carry her tin trunk.'

'What a hope !' said the girl, without lifting her eyes from her book. 'It says here that Drumforber's latitude is 56.51 N. and longitude 2.28 W. It must be somewhere sort of north-east. I wonder if it's big enough to be on the map.'

Said Willie : 'Ach, it'll be yin o' thae wee villages wi' thatched roofs an' a well where a' the weemin gaither fur a gossip when they come oot fur a pail o' watter.'

'Yes,' agreed Peter, speaking from his hiking experience, 'and there'll be one shop where they sell everything from paraffin to red herring.'

'Oh, paraffin !' exclaimed Sarah. 'That reminds me—I've heard of country people coming to the town and blowing out the gas—the same as they would do with a candle. It's a good thing we've got electric light. I'll need to watch she doesn't go near the gas-cooker.'

At that moment Maisie found the place on the map and proceeded to demonstrate that it lay between the Grampians and the sea, south of Aberdeen.

'I wonder if this'll be the first time she'll ever have been on a train ?' said Peter. 'I feel less and less like going to meet her. What about you going, Dad ?'

'Nae fear ! Ma chilblains is botherin' me. Hoo auld will she be, Serah ?'

Sarah had to think before coming to the conclusion that the girl would be about twenty-four.

'Twenty-four !' said Maisie. 'What kind of job can she be going in for in one of the hospitals ? She can't be starting to train as a nurse at that age !'

'Maybe she's going to be a ward-maid or a cleaner,' suggested

Sarah. 'Come on, Peter, you better get dressed for going to the station. I'll need Maisie to help me to get her room ready. All the same, I think Bella might have given us a bit more notice than this.'

'Don't forget the lassie's bringin' eggs, Serah.' The reminder came from her husband. 'D'ye think they've got a wee farm?'

'The last I heard of Bella's husband was, he was a plumber in Aberdeen.'

'He'll be drawin' the dole noo, then,' said Willie. 'There's no' much can go wrang wi' a village well.'

But Sarah's mind was off on another tack. 'Oh, Maisie,' she exclaimed, 'could you not give Peter one of your old coats to take to the station, and if Sheena turns out to be awful outlandishly dressed, he could get her to put on your coat.'

Peter demanded, 'Who said I was going to the station? I think, seeing it's a girl, it would be far better if either you or Maisie went.'

'But I've just told you—Maisie and I have too much to do.' Sarah turned her back on her son. 'Maisie—away you and strip your bed. I'll look out clean sheets and things.'

'Listen, Mother,' protested Maisie, 'I think we've time to get Matt's room ready. I don't want to share my bed with a girl that'll likely be stinking to high heaven with hen's meat and candle-grease.'

'We'll make her take a bath as soon as she arrives. That's bound to be a treat for her. Maybe she's got to wash in a burn every morning. Come on, Peter. Get your coat on.'

Secretly the lad was intrigued by the thought of a strange girl coming to live in the home, but he continued his show of resistance while obediently putting on his coat.

'When ye come tae think o't,' said Willie, 'there'll be an awfu' lota things in Glesca tae take 'er braith away. There'll be the tramcaurs an' the streets wi' lichts in them . . .'

'And the shops!' Maisie suddenly became enthusiastic. 'Mother, you and I will have the time of our lives taking her along Sauchiehall Street.'

4

'I think Argyle Street'll be nearer her level,' retorted Sarah. 'Unless of course she gets frightened for the crowds.'

'Ay here, Peter,' said Willie, 'she'll maybe ask ye tae take 'er intae a shop door tae the crood goes by at the station.'

Peter ignored the remark while Maisie allowed her imagination to run loose over the field of Sheena's probable ignorance about city flats, which in turn raised another worry in Sarah's mind.

'Oh,' she said, 'maybe she'll not sleep for the noise of the traffic.'

'That's another reason for putting her in Matt's room,' said Maisie. 'It's at the back.'

'Ay, but whit aboot the men empyin' the ashbins through the night?' asked her father. 'She'll think it's bombs or somethin'.'

Sarah dismissed the idea with her contention that Drumforber was too much in the heart of the country for the girl to have had any experience of the noise of a bomb. This picture of isolation caused Peter to say, as he pulled on his gloves, 'She'll not have seen a policeman either.'

'Naw, nur a Lord Provost even,' added Willie.

'Or the pictures!' In her glee at the prospect, Maisie slapped her brother's back. 'Peter, my lad, you'll have to take her to the pictures.'

'I will not! I'll not know where to hide myself when she shouts out "Mind yer back, mister!"'

'She'll no' speak like that!' objected Willie. 'She'll speak like Harry Gordon—wi' an Aiberdeen accent.'

'So she will,' agreed his wife; then, remembering an old grievance, she added, 'She'll never be able to make you out, Willie, unless you speak proper.'

In disgust Willie retired from the conversation with: 'Ach, lea'e me alane!'

About an hour later, Sarah was satisfied that there was at least a clean bed for the visitor to share with Maisie, and Maisie for her part was satisfied that the *lingerie* she had unwrapped from

5

its tissue paper would astound Sheena when they were both undressing that night. Returning to the kitchen they were greeted with a speculative query from Willie :

' Hoo mony eggs d'ye think the lassie'll bring ye, Serah ? Ah could dae wi' a feed o' ham an' eggs—three eggs.'

' Ugh, you, you've got nothing in your head but your stomach ! '

' The first time ye said that,' replied Willie in disgust, ' Ah thought ye were tryin' tae be funny, but——'

His observations were cut short by Sarah's warning: ' Shsh ! I think I hear them on the stair.' In a moment there was a peal on the doorbell.

' Maisie,' said Sarah, ' you come to the door with me and we'll take her to your room first. I hope the bath water is hot enough.'

When the preliminary greetings were over, Peter found his way to the kitchen, closed the door and whispered, ' Dad ! You should see Cousin Sheena ! Boy, what a smasher ! All dressed up to the nines, with her face made-up worse than Maisie's. And you should hear her speak. Talk about Pan Loaf ! '

Willie shared twinkles with his son. ' D'ye tell me that ! She widnae hauf caw the feet f'ae Maisie an' yer mither.'

' Oh, but wait till I tell you ! Coming up the stair just now I thought it would be a rare joke to kid on the pair of them. So before we came in Sheena combed out her hair and did it up old-fashioned—you know—with a bun at the back. Then she took all the make-up off her face and tied a woollen scarf round her head.'

' So she's no' a country cousin efter a' ? ' whispered Willie.

' Not a bit of her ! D'you know, I nearly split my sides laughing at the difference in her. She's going to speak like Harry Gordon till I think Mother and Maisie have had enough.'

' Ay ? Ye'll be takin' 'er tae the pictures the night efter a' ? ' queried Willie impishly.

' Sure thing ! '

At that moment the door opened and Willie turned round expectantly, but only his wife and daughter were to be seen.

' She's having a wash-up,' explained Maisie, in answer to her father's inquiry. 'She says she doesn't want to take a bath just now because she always changes her neathies and hasn't got a spare lot with her.'

'Ah could len' 'er a semmit an' dr—— things,' offered Willie with a wink at his son.

Maisie, oblivious to the tense excitement of the males of the household, turned to her mother, saying, 'Did you ever see such a hair-do? A bun—of all things! I'll need to tell her that nobody under ninety wears a bun nowadays. Boy! Am I going to enjoy myself!'

Sarah smiled. 'Isn't it laughable the way she puts " ie " on to everything she says, like " the bussie " and " the roadie." '

As she bustled off to make tea, Willie poked his son in the ribs and said, 'Heh, if she pits " ie " on tae everythin', whit'll she say when the doorbell rings?'

The gale of Peter's laughter followed Sarah into the scullery, whence she uttered her time-worn stricture on vulgarity. She returned to the kitchen with a trayful of cups and saucers, punctuating Peter's laughter with the injunction not to encourage his father.

Willie brushed aside her counsels, peering at the tea-tray. 'Are ye no' gonnae gi'e the lassie a set-doon tea?' he demanded.

'No,' said Sarah. 'For one thing she's not hungry, she says. She had a softie in the trainie. And for another she's just dying to get out to the pictures.' Turning sympathetically to Peter, she went on, 'I'm awful sorry, son, that you've got to take her, but just try to think of the grand time Sheena will have. After all, it's dark outside and nobody'll see how she's dressed.'

Peter turned aside to hide his sniggers, glad of Maisie's unconscious help when she expressed the opinion that the oatmeal coat wasn't too bad, it was just the way it was worn that made it look so gawky. Suddenly the door opened and Sheena stood with exaggerated awkwardness trying to avoid looking at her fellow conspirator.

'Come over to the fire,' urged Maisie.

Willie got to his feet. 'Hoo' ye, Sheena?' said he, with an outstretched hand.

7

Sheena grasped it heartily. 'Foo are ye, Uncle Willie?' she bawled with equal heartiness.

'Fine, thanks,' said Willie. 'Are ye no' caul' comin' aff the train?'

'Na-na,' was the reply. 'I'm nae cal' ava.' Then, catching sight of Peter's attempts to choke his laughter, she rushed into further and broader speech. 'Eh me, but I'm forgettin'. My Mam gi'ed me a curran thingies for ye, Auntie Sarah. I hae them in my baggie. I'll get them for ye.'

The girl found temporary respite in the darkness of the lobby, while Maisie cast her eyes towards the clothes-poles on the ceiling and declaimed, 'Suffering snakes, she's got something in her baggie!'

Her father grinned. 'Ah wonder if it's got onythin' tae dae wi' a baggie-meenie?' he asked, adding, with a prod of his foot, 'Eh, Peter?'

Peter blew his nose elaborately and conceded that Sheena was a star turn. In a moment or two she was back in their midst, saying:

'Here ye are, Auntie Sarah. My Mam said I was to tell ye that this is jist a wee hennie an' it'll roast brawly.'

Sarah gaped with pleasure at the untidy parcel that was handed over.

'An' twa-three eggies,' went on Sheena, as she dived again into her shopping bag.

'Twa-three?' repeated Sarah. 'Goodness, there must be a dozen here. I don't remember seeing so many all together at one time for years. Are you sure this isn't Black Market?'

'Na-na,' insisted Sheena, turning a staunch back on her nose-blowing cousin. 'We hae nae mair nor twenty hennies, so we're nae controlled. An' here's a pucklie odds an' ends—some farm butter, some shorties, a packettie oatcakes an' a jar o' run-honey.'

Sarah received the gifts wide-eyed. 'Oh dear-dear,' she exclaimed. 'Did you folk in Drumforber know there was a war on?'

'Oh fairly ay, min. Fairly ay ! We kent it wis ower onywye, for the mannie gaed alang the roadie ringin' 'is bell. . . .'

'" ie " ' added Willie to her last word.

Wilfully misunderstanding the spelling of his interjection, Sheena repeated her statement that a mannie had gaed alang the roadie.

'It's all right, Sheena,' said Peter, finding his voice at length. 'Dad heard you the first time. What happened when the mannie rang the bell—eh ? '

Sheena simulated a pout. ' Ye're makkin' a feel o' me, Peter.'

' Don't heed him,' said Maisie. ' Go on with your story.'

' We hed a bone-fyer at the tap o' the hill, an' we a' gaed up till't on larries, an' we hed a band, an' some o's wis dancin'.'

' Dancing ? ' said Maisie, still condescending. ' The Highland fling and all that, I suppose ? '

' Na-na. We hed mod-ren dancin'.'

Once again Maisie appealed to the clothes-poles. ' I'd like,' she said with solemn supplication, ' to hear boogie-woogie on the bagpipes. Or would I ? '

The teapot was produced and Sarah urged her visitor to sit down near the fire, but Sheena had one more gift to present. It was, she said, a cakie that her Mam had baked.

Sarah uncovered it, sniffing its excellence. ' Oh, it smells lovely,' she burst out. ' Fancy, I wouldn't 've thought there would've been ovens in Drumforber that could have baked a cake like this. Is it a paraffin one your mother has ? '

' Na-na,' said Sheena ; ' it's a coal een.' As though to banish from her memory her mother's latest model of cream-enamelled stoves, the girl fingered the tray-cloth. ' My ! ' she exclaimed, ' this is an affa fine clothie, Auntie Sarah. Did ye mak it yersel'?'

' I did that,' said Sarah. ' I used to do a lot of crochet.'

' Wis't a fikey jobbie ? '

' A what ? '

Willie stepped into the breach. ' Here, Sheena, lass, yer auntie's needin' tae go back tae school tae learn braid Scots. Sit ye doon here aside me. Whit'll ye hae tae eat ? '

The girl sat down beside her uncle and, ignoring the plateful of pancakes he held out to her, she clasped her hands and eyed him soulfully. ' Eh, Uncle Willie,' she said, ' I like affa weel to hear ye speak.'

The other three gasped ' What ! ' in unison, and with such conviction that Sheena demanded, ' Fit's a-dee ?   Do you-lads nae like the wye he speaks ?   He minds me on somebody on the wireless.'

' Not an announcer, I'll bet ! ' said Maisie.

' Na-na.   Mair like een o' thae wee comics.   Fit's 'is name again ? . . .'

Sarah cut into the girl's reminiscences of wireless comics with the remark : ' So you've got the wireless in Drumforber !   I wouldn't 've thought you'd 've known what the wireless was ! '

Sheena swallowed hard and, like Peter, reached for her handkerchief.

' I suppose it'll be a one-teacher school,' said Maisie.

Truth triumphed as Sheena admitted that the educational outlook was of greater scope than that encompassed by the activities of one teacher, but added quickly, ' Foo mony teachers is there in your skweel ? '

' Oh, between sixty and seventy,' replied Maisie off-handedly.

' Gweedsakes ! ' was all that Sheena could trust herself to say.

While the teacups were being handed round Peter found sufficient self-control to ask, ' What size of a place is Drumforber —one street and a village well ? '

' Oh, we hae mair than jist the ae street.   An' we hae a squarie wi' grass growin' on't.'

' Whit's the squarie fur ? ' asked Willie.   ' Turnin' the coos ontae when ye're muckin' oot the byre ? '

' Oh, the loons play on't, filies.   Last year we hed an affa fine do on't.   A fancy-dress fitba' match—ae team wis loons dressed up as affa al'-fashioned wifies, an' the ither team wis quinies dressed up as loons wi' fitba' jerseys an' pantics.   Of course it wisnae a fitba' match ava, ye ken.   It wis jist a wye-o'-deein'.'

' A what ? ' demanded Sarah.

' A wye-o'-deein',' repeated Sheena distinctly.

Sarah suddenly became aware of her son's facial contortions.
' Peter ! ' she exclaimed indignantly, ' don't sit there giggling
like a schoolgirl. You're very rude.' Then, as if to compensate
the visitor for the lad's rudeness, she went on, ' Peter's looking
forward to taking you to the pictures. That'll be a treat for
you, won't it ? '

' It will that ! ' agreed Sheena, looking earnestly at her half-
nibbled pancake. To her relief the family then occupied themselves with a lengthy and heated discussion as to the most suitable
film to which she should be taken. Finally, the decision reached,
her hostess urged her to get ready for the outing, adding as an
afterthought :

' Ehm . . . are you sure your coat is warm enough ? Maisie
could lend you one of hers, if you like. A real smart one it
is ! '

' Na-na. I'll nae be cal' if I'm to be hotterin' ower the steens
followin' Peter. He flees along the roadie like stoor, ye ken.
Of coorse he's as like as no' ashamed o' 'is country cousin an'
doesna want fowk tae ken he's along wi' her.'

This Peter vehemently denied as Maisie persuaded the girl to
go to her room and dress. When the door had closed and the
family were by themselves again, Maisie exclaimed :

' Boy, she's not half going to get an eye-opener at the pictures ! ' She allowed her imagination to run away with her.
' Just fancy what she'll 've been used to—probably a flannelette
sheet pinned up in the village hall, with a magic lantern worked
by two candles and a bicycle lamp. I nearly wish I was going
with you, Peter.'

Peter viewed the suggestion with disfavour. ' I've taken this
on,' he pointed out with almost overdone missionary zeal, ' and
I'm doing it on my own.'

' I'm real proud of you,' said Sarah, ' but never mind, son.
After Maisie's taken her in hand she'll be quite presentable.'

' I'll get to work on her hair first,' Maisie promised herself and her family. ' It looks clean enough, but I'll give her
a shampoo first and then try out different styles.'

Her mother joined in enthusiastically in proposing schemes for the improvement of the visitor, until Willie asked mildly if they didn't think Sheena might be pulling their leg.

'What!' demanded Maisie; 'that wee bannock pulling our leg? Not on your life! She's a nice enough girl, I admit, but all the same. . . .'

'She's an awful lot nicer than I expected,' said Sarah. 'She makes you feel you want to—to sort of mother her, doesn't she?'

'I wonder if she'd faint at the sight of lipstick,' said Maisie. 'I'd like to experiment with her face.'

'The lassie's face is fine!' blurted out her father. 'You lea'e it alane! The muck you pit on your face jist aboot gi'es me the bo——'

'Willie!' shouted his wife.

'Well, make's me seek, then, if ye think that's mair refined.'

Sarah fetched her purse and, extracting two half-crowns, she attempted to push them into Peter's hand, saying, 'That'll help to pay you and Sheena into the pictures.'

Peter returned the coins indignantly, insisting that he wanted to pay for Sheena himself—a statement that roused his mother's suspicions.

'Here—what's up with you?' she demanded. 'I've never known you to refuse money before. There's something funny going on, and I'd like to know what it is. You sat there all the time we were having tea and giggled like an idiot. Come on—out with it!'

But before confession had been dragged out of Peter the door opened, and a smart young lady stood there saying, in the pleasantest of standard English accents, 'Well, Peter, I'm ready.'

Everybody gasped—even Peter. Sarah was the first to find her voice.

'Sheena!' she gulped. 'What have you done to yourself?'

'My sainted aunt!' said Maisie. 'What a transformation!'

Sheena patted her sleek coiffure and smiled condescendingly on her cousin. 'Oh, no, Maisie, it's not a transformation—it's all my own hair.'

'You—you've changed!' insisted Sarah. 'You're just not

the same girl!' She contemplated the artifice applied to her niece's face and continued, 'What would your mother say if she saw you with all that lipstick on?'

Sheena shrugged her shoulders. 'I'm afraid Mother wouldn't recognise me without it.' She brought a slim cigarette case from her handbag, opened it and offered the contents to Maisie. Maisie declined with a shake of a bewildered head.

'But what's come over you?' went on Sarah as the girl flicked a lighter into operation, and blinked in sophisticated nonchalance through the smoke. 'It's not just your lipstick and your—your cigarette, it's your hair and your clothes and everything. You'll never get a job as a cleaner in a Glasgow hospital if you go all dolled up like that for your interview.'

'Who's wanting a job as a cleaner?' asked the visitor in genuine amazement.

'I thought that's what . . .' began Sarah. Swallowing, she tried again : 'Well, what *are* you seeing the matron about?'

'Oh, it's a scheme I've had in mind for a long time. After I took my Arts degree at Aberdeen University——'

'Your Arts degree?' spluttered Maisie.

'I didn't like the idea of teaching,' went on Sheena, unperturbed, 'so I went to London for a couple of years—to the Academy of Music, and took my L.R.'

'So you're L.R.A.M. as well?' Maisie could not hide her astonishment.

'Does that mean you could tune our piano for us?' asked Sarah, only to be shushed by her blushing daughter.

'Oh, it's not a musical degree I've got,' explained Sheena. 'It's for elocution. I once thought of going on the stage, you know.'

'The stage!' gasped Sarah.

'But I finally decided I'd take a course in Occupational Therapy.'

'Whit kinna beast is that?' inquired Willie.

'Oh, you must have heard of it. The Government is doing quite a lot of it under their Rehabilitation Schemes. That's what I'm seeing matron about on Monday. I'd like to start a clinic on my own if she turns down my rather revolutionary ideas on the subject.'

Still unconvinced, Sarah tried recrimination : ' But what was the idea of kidding us on you were a—a country bumpkin ? '

' Oh, well, I'm afraid that was mean of me, but you see, you were all so determined that Drumforber wore its hair in a bun that I thought I'd live up to your standards for a bit. Peter knew.'

' You're a wee marvel ! ' Peter was sincere in his congratulations, but impatient to be out and about with this gorgeous creature who seemed so out of place in a workaday kitchen. ' Come on, it's time we were moving.'

But his father was thirsting for more information. ' So Drumforber's no' a wee village efter a' ? '

' Hardly,' smiled Sheena. ' It's got five hotels—or pubs, to be more truthful—a picture-house, gas-works, to say nothing of the provost, magistrates and town councillors.'

' Huh,' grinned her uncle. ' Whi' d'ye want wi' a gas-works if ye've got a toon cooncil ? '

' And,' added Sheena, ' it's better lit than some of the Glasgow streets I've seen.'

' You're certainly one of the shining lights of the place, anyway,' conceded Maisie.

' Thank you, Maisie . . . well, Peter, shall we go ? '

' You bet ! ' Peter's coat was already half on.

At the door Sheena turned. ' Oh, Maisie, when I was in London I took a course in hairdressing. When we come back from the pictures I'll give you a shampoo and reset your hair. That style you're wearing went out about three months ago. See you anon, folks.'

The door was closed and Maisie was left staring at it. ' Ye gods ! ' she gulped. ' *She's* going to do *my* hair ! '

CHAPTER 2

UNDER CANVAS

SHEENA'S presence in the house over the week-end brightened the family's spirits considerably, and all four were keenly interested in the outcome of her talk with the matron. When she arrived back at the McFlannel flat on the Monday forenoon with the news that she had got the post at the hospital, no-one could have been more delighted than her Aunt Sarah. The girl took up permanent residence at the hospital, but much of her off-duty time was spent with her cousins, and as was to be expected Sarah and her sister Bella renewed acquaintance with each other by regular correspondence.

Between Bella McJute's letters and Sheena's enthusiasm for her home townlet there emerged the impression that Drumforber must be rather an exceptional place, both for beauty of scenery and for abundance of food ; consequently when the question of holidays arose it was only natural that their thoughts should turn to the Howe o' the Mearns. Sarah was urged to find out from her sister what the prospects were of there being accommodation for them in some house in the village, but the reply was to the effect that neither she, Bella, nor any other woman in Drumforber could put at their disposal three bedrooms and a living-room.

They had all set their hearts so much on seeing the place that when Peter suggested a camping holiday the proposal was not turned down by Sarah with such alacrity as might have been expected from a woman of her conservative nature. Willie, for his part, hailed the idea with delight ; he was, he contended, a dab-hand at camp cookery as a result of the 1914-18 war. Maisie was more guarded in her attitude, and secretly arranged an alternative holiday with a girl friend, determining to spend only the week-ends at Drumforber.

In early September, then, on a Friday afternoon, Willie and Peter made the journey north by themselves in order to get the camp ready for the arrival of Sarah and Maisie the following day. They took with them, *inter alia*, a tent which they had acquired through the comprehensive agency of Uncle Mattha. They found a likely-looking field near the station and got to work, dispensing with the formality of asking permission to do so. The tent, when unwrapped and laid on the grass, proved to be as Uncle Mattha had promised, of the cottage type ; too late they realised that its moth-eaten appearance had been glossed over by that man of business. Happy as a boy scout at his first camp, however, Willie pooh-poohed each deficiency pointed out by Peter, and Sarah would scarcely have recognised her agile husband darting to and fro among the guy-ropes and not once becoming entangled therewith.

When everything was in order Willie dusted his hands on the seat of his trousers and bethought him of the empty condition of his stomach. He had been boasting for days about his skill as a camp cook, but the present problem of first catching his hare caused him to decide on a meal in a restaurant. Sitting down in the back shop of a baker's premises, they drummed on the table until one of the shop assistants was compelled to look in their direction.

' Is there ony chance o' gettin' twa eggs wi' a plate o' ham ? ' asked Willie.

' Sorry.'

' Fish and chips, then ? ' asked Peter, with an appraising look at the girl's neat figure.

' Sorry.'

' Well, we'll make one egg dae wi' the ham,' said Willie, interested only in his own figure.

The girl shook her head. ' We can just give you a hot pie,' she said.

' Whit ! No' even cauld meat ? '

' Sorry.'

' Aw, here, miss, we were tellt that Drumforber wis a land flowin' wi' milk an' honey.'

' Sorry, this is a baker's shop, not a dairy.'

Father and son exchanged glances. ' Let's go to one of the five hotels Sheena bragged about.'

' Naw, Ah'm no' dressed fur nae hotels. Is this the only tea-room in the place, miss ? '

' Yes.'

' Is there no' even a fish-an'-chip shop ? '

' Oh, yes.' The girl refused to succumb to Peter's eyebrow gestures, adding dispassionately, ' But it doesn't open till eight o'clock.'

' Bring on the pies, then,' said Willie. ' Twa each an' yin fur the plate.'

But the pie situation could not cope with such a wholesale order, and the deficiency had to be made up with bread of which there was plenty, and real butter to spread on it. Then, feeling less hungry, the two holiday-makers strolled aimlessly up and down the main street, obeying to the letter Sarah's instructions that they were not to call on Aunt Bella until officially invited to do so. The exact position of the fish-and-chip shop being ascertained, they wandered about until they found the public park, where they played at putting until the heavy mist that was blanketing out the view turned to rain. For a couple of hours they sat in the fish-and-chip shop talking to the locals and being talked to by drivers of fish lorries en route from and to Aberdeen. Carrying a further supply of cooked fish and potatoes in the shelter of their oxters, they plunged through puddles and driving rain to their camp. There the scene was so wretched that, having placed pails and basins beneath the largest of the holes in Uncle Mattha's tent, they packed a small suitcase with pyjamas and plunged forth once more in the direction of the burgh of Drum-forber. It was by now almost eleven o'clock, and the first hotel refused to open its doors to them ; three others said flatly that visitors were not accommodated ; the fifth was so humble that even Willie did not feel self-conscious when invited to come in.

The next morning not even the weird design of the pseudo-wallpaper in the dining-room could rob them of their enjoyment of the huge plateful of ham and eggs that was placed before each of them. Though the weather had by now improved, their chief worry was how to conceal the real state of affairs from Sarah and Maisie when they arrived.

'One thing's certain,' said Peter; 'we'd better keep it dark that we've spent the night in the Gardenside Hotel.'

Together they returned to the camp, emptied the basins and pails that had been filled to overflowing in their absence, and viewed the blue sky with increasing tranquillity.

On the station platform Peter remarked that it would have been advisable to stow away the pails and basins instead of replacing them where they had stood all night.

'Don't fash,' said his father. 'We'll jist say we pit them there tae cover rat holes.'

'How would that help? Is Mother fond of rats?'

'Nane o' yer lip.' Willie was by now in a state of eager expectancy—not so much of the pleasure of the company of his wife and daughter as that of the Cairn terrier which had recently taken the place of Lassie. 'Ah hope,' he went on, 'that Susan hasnae been seek in the train. Ah'm fair wearyin' tae see the wee dug again.' As the train steamed into the station he added, 'Noo mind—keep yer trap shut aboot the Gardenside Hotel !'

For the next few minutes there was no need to fear conversational *gaucheries*, for they were kept running from one end of the platform to the other in search of the guard's van; then, having found it and with the porter's help extracted the hamper, Willie committed the unpardonable sin of welcoming the dog that was prancing round his feet to the neglect of his wife and daughter.

Sarah's jealousy found expression. 'You're a fine one—never even look to see if Maisie and I are all right.'

Willie glanced perfunctorily at his women-folk. 'Hoo'ye,' he said impartially to them both; then to Sarah, 'Ye're no' ony thinner than when Ah seen ye yesterday.'

Maisie prodded him with a sharp corner of her suitcase :

'I'm here too, Dad. Would you scratch my head if I got down on my hands and knees and wiggled my tail?'

'Don't be vulgar, Maisie. Is the tent near the station, Peter?'

'It's just round the corner, Mother,' said the lad. 'Right opposite the gas-works there.'

'The gas-works!' cried mother and daughter simultaneously. 'What a place to put a tent! The smell'll be awful.'

'Ach ay,' said Willie, still giving more than half his attention to the dog that was running ahead in glee; 'but ye don't notice it when Peter takes aff 'is shoes.'

They moved off in a body. 'Did you get the tent up all right?' asked Sarah.

The casualness of Willie's 'Ay, oh ay' was rather overdone, but Sarah was too anxious to be assured of their having aired the blankets thoroughly before they slept in them to notice his manner.

'Oh, we slep' in the Garden . . .' began Willie reassuringly, when he remembered he ought not to have mentioned the matter. He breenged into a change of subject. 'Here, Peter, Ah'll gi'e ye a hand wi' that hamper, an' we'll no' need a porter.'

But his ruse was not entirely successful, for Maisie pounced on his earlier topic: 'What was the idea—sleeping in a garden?'

'Ah never sayed nothin' aboot sleepin' in a gairden. Serah, see's me that case. It's ower heavy fur ye.'

'How do you know?' was the ungrateful response. 'In any case I've got some pots of jam in it, and I can't trust you. Why did you not sleep in the tent?'

Peter rallied to his father's help: 'Mother—look! Look at the lovely view. That's Finella Hill—and see yonder—the road winding up the hill beyond it—Cairn o' Mount, it's called. It goes right over to Banchory and Deeside.'

Sarah fell into the trap. 'I didn't expect to see so many hills,' she said with real pleasure. 'I always imagined the east of Scotland was flat.'

Maisie, however, was not unaware of the undercurrent of secrecy. 'Yes, but, Peter, why did you sleep——'

It was Willie's turn now to act as cicerone of the red-herring.

He pointed dramatically in the opposite direction. 'Thon's Garvock Hill,' he explained. 'The sea's jist at the ither side. They say ye get a rare view f'ae thon Tower.'

Sarah looked at her husband searchingly. 'Were you so busy collecting all this information that you couldn't make up your beds in the tent last night?'

Once again it was Peter's turn. 'Oh, Mother, you'll never guess! There's a van comes three times a week with fish—line caught—from a wee fishing village about ten miles away. And there's a fish shop in the main street!'

'Very appropriate!' observed Maisie. 'There's something fishy about this sleeping-in-a-garden business.'

Just then they found themselves at the gate of the gas-works and the tent itself hove in sight. To offset any criticism his wife might have to make on the subject of the position of the tent, Willie hastened to explain that it had been placed there so that she could sit inside and have an uninterrupted view of the hills.

'In't it no' a grand view?' he wheedled. 'Thae's the foot-hills o' the Grampians. An' Glen Esk is ower thonder—see?'

But Sarah refused to look in the direction of his pointing finger. 'All I can see—and smell—is the gas-works.'

Maisie's eyes dwelt on the tent. 'Mercy, what a size!' she commented.

'Dad and I have got it all curtained off into rooms,' said Peter. 'We've even got flowers for the table.'

'I'll do without flowers,' put in Sarah, 'if I can be sure of a decent stove for cooking on. Is it working all right?'

Willie exchanged a look of uncertainty with his son. 'Ay, oh ay. Ehm . . . it's makin' a bit o' a smell, but ach, ye'll get used wi't.'

The procession moved through the gate and over the damp grass to the tent. En route, Maisie asked why they had had to sleep in a garden, seeing that the accommodation had been so carefully roped off. But the uncomfortable moment passed, thanks to Susan, who suddenly disappeared. Her whereabouts, however, were soon indicated by the waving of the rushes in a nearby ditch. Sarah was afraid she would come to grief.

' Ach, she's fine ! ' Willie assured her. ' She'll be efter a rat.'

' Oh—a rat ! I'm terrified of the things.'

' Ye'll get used wi' them. Look at the wey ye've got used wi' me.'

Sarah dismissed the assertion with a sniff, then, fixing her eyes on the slopes of Finella Hill, she asked if there were any shops in the place.

' Oh,' said Peter, ' there's bags of shops along the main street. There's even a fish-and-chip shop.'

' Allow you and Dad to find that out ! ' exclaimed Maisie. ' I'll bet that's where you and Dad were last night before you went to sleep in the Garden of Mystery.'

Sarah rounded on them. ' Yes, here ! Why did you two not sleep in the tent ? '

' Here—get inside an' we'll explain. Coorie doon or ye'll get yer hat cawed aff yer heid.'

Sarah, bending, announced halfway through the tent flap that it was stuffy and dark.

' Except,' added Maisie, following her, and nearly tripping over a pail, ' right under that hole in the roof. What's it for ? '

Peter cleared his throat, swallowed, then answered bravely that it was for ventilation, and would she come and see her ' room ' ? ' Look,' he raised a corner of the groundsheet curtain, ' this is Dad and Mother's section. This is the only corner where there's room for two camp beds.' He raised another flap. ' I'm in here, see ? ' Maisie, seeing, passed on to the next curtain. ' This is your boudoir,' said Peter.

' Just a minute,' said she, having examined the last two sections. ' I think I prefer your corner.'

' Just as you like, but it's only fair to tell you that the bit I earmarked for you is the only place in the tent where there's not a rat-hole.'

' A rat-hole ? ' she gasped.

' Yes, that's what all the basins are on the ground for—to cover the rat-holes.'

Maisie peered into her allotted portion again. ' Thu—thu—there's a saucer on the floor here ! '

' Oh, that would just be a mouse-hole. But I'm not frightened for mice. I'll swap rooms with you.'

For a moment Maisie studied his face, then she burst out laughing. ' You're a fiend, Peter. You had me fooled there ! What *are* all the basins for ? '

' Look up and you'll see. Uncle Mattha's tent is riddled with holes. It was raining cats and dogs last night, and we had to sleep in a hotel.'

' And where did the garden come in ? '

' There was no garden. The name of the hotel is The Garden-side.'

' I'll make a note of that—it might come in handy. I take it you don't want Mother to know the tent's leaking ? '

' No, Dad's so keen on a camping holiday he's scared anything happens to bust it up. It'll be okay if the weather holds.'

Their father's voice interrupted them : ' Hiv you got Susan in there aside you ? '

' No,' answered Peter. ' I haven't seen her since we came into the tent.'

Instantly Willie was in a froth of concern for the dog's safety. He ran out yelling, ' Susan ! Susan ! Come on an' get somethin' tae eat ! '

' Don't say that, Willie,' Sarah called after him. ' I haven't got my case opened yet. You shouldn't tell lies—not even to a dog.'

Rushing to the tent door, Maisie shouted teasingly, ' Are you sure she's not down one of your rat-holes, Dad ? ' Then, ignoring the look of horror on her mother's face, she went back to her ' boudoir,' emerging only when she had dressed herself in raiment she felt suitable to the occasion. Willie, returning to see if Susan had come back during his absence, gaped at the result.

' Jeengs ! ' he ejaculated. ' Wha's troosers is thae ? '

' They're my own, Dad. And they're called slacks.'

' I hope,' said Sarah, ' that the Drumforber people don't get a shock when they see you.'

' They'd get mair o' a shock if they seen *you* in slacks, Serah.' He turned to go out on a further search for the dog when he nearly collided with a burly fresh-faced man carrying it in his arms. 'There ye are, lass!' he gurgled with delight and relief.

'Well-well,' said the stranger, by way of greeting.

'It's a grand evenin',' replied Willie.

'It is that! So you're tentin'?'

'Ay. We've aye had a notion tae hae a campin' holiday, an' we didnae get away at the Fair this year wi' the staggerin' o' the holidays at the shipyaird, so here we are.'

'Ye'll be frae Glasgow?'

'That's right. Hoo did ye know?'

'Oh, somethin' aboot the wye ye speak, min. I hae nae mind o' gettin' a letter frae onybody in Glasgow askin' permission to put up a tent, though.'

Willie paused in his stroking of Susan's head to say, 'Ah never thocht. Are we trespassin'?'

'Well, in a manner o' speakin' ye are, min.'

Inside the tent Sarah clutched at her beads and, with visions of imprisonment, whispered, 'Oh dear-dear. Is he going to prosecute us?' But the farmer was speaking again.

'This'll be your bitchie?' He held the dog up.

'Ay. That's Susan. A quiet wee beast, she is.'

'She was chasin' my cattle-beasts ee-noo.'

Willie apologised. 'If ye'll jist let 'er aff for a first offence, mister, Ah'll promise ye she'll no' dae it again. It's jist the chynge f'ae thae gullies o' streets in Glesca. She's fair divertit —like wursels.'

The man handed over the wriggling Susan. 'Well-well, we'll forget a' aboot it this time. Is this yer first campin' do?'

'Oh well,' Willie nuzzled his face into his dog's neck. 'Ah got a wee taste o't in the last war.'

'Ay? Fit regiment?'

'The 9th H.L.I.'

'Let me see—the 9th was the Glasgow Highlanders, was't no'?'

'Ay—the guid auld G.H. Wis you away yersel'?'

'Ay, min. I was in the Gordons.'

'Ach, whit made ye go intae a mob like the Gordons? Ye shoulda jined the sodgers!'

In the dusky background Sarah was still fumbling with her neckwear. 'Oh, what a thing to say to the man!' she wailed.

'They tell me,' went on the farmer, 'that the G.H. used to take their pyjamas into the trenches.'

'So Ah've heard. An' they tell me that the Gordons had tae get kissed by a duchess afore they could be made tae jine up.'

'Oh dear-dear, we'll get prosecuted all right, Maisie,' continued Sarah, on hearing this last retort. 'Why can't your father be civil to the man?'

'Wait you—the farmer can hold his own,' replied Maisie. 'I'm enjoying this.'

'Fit aboot thon tartan your lot wore?' queried the farmer. 'Black Watch—eh?'

'Oh, we'll let that flea stick to the wa',' returned Willie.

'Fit's yer name, min?'

'McFlannel. Whit's yours?'

'Oh, I'm TT.'

'I'm TT masel', but Ah didnae mean that.'

'The name's McCord. Well-well, I'll hae tae be gaein'. Ye'll mind an' keep an' eye on yer doggie?'

'Ah will that.'

'D'ye like rabbit?' He held up a brace of the species.

'Heh, Serah,' called Willie. 'C'm'ere an' see this.'

Sarah advanced timidly and was introduced; Maisie and Peter in turn were also presented, Willie being careful to emphasise the fact that despite appearances only one of them was of the male species. Before he moved off the farmer asked if they played bridge.

'Naw,' said Willie. 'Peter here plays the violin an' Maisie's had two quarters at the pianna, but——'

Maisie cut in with, 'Dad's just trying to be funny, Mr McCord. I'm rather keen on bridge myself.'

'That's grand,' said the farmer. 'Ye'll be needin' some milk. C'wa up to the fermhoose wi' me an' ye'll meet the wife, an' she'll be glad to fix up a game.'

24

'Oh, but you can't go like that!' protested Sarah. 'Those trousers——'

'Dinna fash yersel', Mrs McFlannel. Mrs McCord's got a pair o' these thingies for every day i' the week.'

Sarah watched the two of them go away and turned to berate her husband for his impudence, but he had disappeared.

When night fell they were each in their camp-beds, glad of the one comfort the camp possessed. As for Sarah, never having disguised her dislike of the project, she was now having difficulty disguising her pleasure in the unexpected novelty of it. In the mirk she reached out a questing hand.

'Are you sleeping, Willie?' she murmured.

'Naw. Are you?'

'Isn't it lovely and quiet! No tramcars or buses. No ash-bins being emptied or motor bikes or anything.'

'Ay—it's funny no' tae hear the alarm clock ticking on the mantelpiece.'

'Willie—we'll need to learn to play bridge. We can't have that farmer thinking we're just—just Glesca keelies.'

'Ach away—bridge is fur gentry—no' fur the likes o' you an' me.'

The gentle sough of a rising breeze fell sweetly on the woman's ears. 'D'you hear that, Willie? Isn't it peaceful! Like—like a quiet organ.'

'Here, you better watch yersel', lass, or ye'll be writin' poetry next.'

A solitary lamb bleated in the next field. 'My, isn't that touching! It'll likely be a wee baby lamb crying for its mother.'

'Away wi' ye! There's nae baby lambs at this time o' the year.'

For a few minutes there was complete silence, both within and without the tent. Then an owl hooted in the nearby wood.

'Oh, what was that?' Sarah sat up in fear.

'Ach, lie doon, wumman. It wis jist a hoolet cryin' coo-hooey tae its lawd.'

Once again there was silence, until a sudden gust of wind made the slack tent roof flap like the crack of a whip. And once again Sarah sat up in fear. ' Willie ! 'she pleaded, ' don't let the tent come down on top of us.'

' There's nothin' tae get scared fur, lass,' said the man tenderly enough. ' Tent's aye dae that in the night.'

Fascinated, Sarah watched the ghost-like folds of the canvas billow and sag. The wind, rising yet higher, played on the trees of the wood like a mad musician, so that the cathedral of field and sky was filled with the organ notes. In the lulls between the wind's mightiest diapasons the solitary lamb sang a solo once more, and, its recitative rendered, a vast chorus of other lambs and sheep broke forth into singing.

When the anthem, with full organ accompaniment, was at its loudest, a light appeared through the curtains. Sarah shrieked.

' It's all right, Mother,' called Peter. ' I'm going to make you a cup of tea.'

' Oh, my, that's real kind of you, Peter. Surely it's not just the wind that's making that noise.'

' Some of it's sheep. I heard there's to be a sale of them at the Mart on Monday—there's a hundred or two of them just across the railway line.'

But the explanation did nothing to lessen the volume of sound. Down in the hollow beyond the station another contribution was added to the vocal and instrumental programme, for a railway engine whistled screamingly before charging through the cutting at the head of a long line of goods wagons. Behemoth seemed abroad. From her corner came the amused voice of Maisie singing, ' Oh, it's quiet down here ! '

Yet, miraculously, they were all asleep within an hour. Suddenly it was eight o'clock. Sarah examined her watch, shook it in disbelief, then, realising that her men-folk were attending to the breakfast with all the enthusiasm of boys, she snuggled down among the blankets again. The air was calm, the sunshine was bright ; there was no doorstep to scrub, no brasses to polish ; this, she told herself, was going to be a really restful holiday.

Maisie, in slacks, went for the milk.

CHAPTER 3

HOTEL DÉBUT

A FORTNIGHT passed in idyllic weather. Peter and Maisie spent
the two week-ends at the camp, going back to Glasgow between
times—Peter to his work and Maisie to stay with a friend. Sarah
and her sister refreshed each other's memories of their childhood,
leaving their husbands to drift along to the bowling green. But
now it was Thursday of their last week at Drumforber, and
Sarah sat writing at the shaky all-purpose table at the door of
the tent.

'Whit's this ye're writin' ?.' asked her husband. 'Yer will ?'

'No, it's a letter to Maisie.'

'Well, hurry up. Ye promised tae go a walk wi' me—an'
the dug.'

'I'm just finishing. This is what I've said, " Dear Maisie,
I hope you got home safe on Monday morning. Well, our
camping holiday is nearly over, and your father and I thought
that for a treat we might spend the last week-end in a hotel.
We are tired of camp chairs and things——" '

'Speak fur yersel'. Camp chairs suit me doon tae the grun'
—specially thon day yin o' them burst when Ah sat doon on it.'

'Oh, be quiet ! ' Sarah resumed her reading : " So I wondered if you would look out your father's best suit and my new
blue frock and slippers and bring them with you at the end of
the week. Tell Peter to bring a shirt that he can wear a tie with.
You will likely have to hunt for it for him, for his drawers will
be all ploughed up as usual." '

She paused, a frown on her forehead, and Willie took the
opportunity to say, ' Ah'm surprised at ye ! '

'How ?'

'Speakin' tae Maisie aboot Peter's underthings.'

'I never said a word about underthings! Here—how do you spell "ploughed" again? Has it a W?'

'Hoo should Ah know?'

'Maisie's so pass-remarkable—especially about letters. Peter and her'll be having a fine laugh at me if I've got any mistakes in grammar.'

'Ach well, ye should speak the Doric—it's got nae grammar. Come on—hurry up wi' that letter. Is there much mair tae go?'

'No. I've just said, "We have managed to get fixed up at the hotel about five miles from here, but they could only give us two rooms, so your father and Peter can have the big bedroom and the small one will do for you and me."'

'Well—that's no' right grammar onywey,' put in Willie. 'It should be "for you and I"—should it no'?'

Once again Sarah's brow was wrinkled. 'D'you think so?' she asked. 'It certainly sounds more genteel. I'd better change it. I don't want my family to be ashamed of me.'

'Ach, ye're fine,' said the man, anxious to be off on his promised walk. Sarah, however, interpreted the remark differently.

'Do you really mean that?' she asked wistfully, so wistfully that Willie, gallantly, blurted out :

'Well, an' whit-fur-no'? Have ye had a guid holiday, lass?'

'I have that, Willie. I never thought it would be so nice—especially during the week when we've just been our two selves.'

'Ah wis jist thinkin' that masel'. Ye havenae been getting on tae me so much.'

'Well, you've been behaving yourself for once.'

'Gie me the simple life every time. Ah could dae fine wi' livin' in a tent fur the rest o' ma natural.'

'Not me!' declared Sarah with conviction. 'I'll be glad to get back to my kitchen sink again.' She folded up the letter with a grim look in the direction of the pails full of water that were so essential to camp life ; there was, she felt, a limit to novelty.

The following Saturday afternoon Sarah took a cursory

glance at the pale swatch of grass on which their tent had stood for a fortnight. She felt sure she would never repeat the experiment, and told herself that she was glad they were going to spend the last week-end in a hotel ; it would at least be something to brag about to Mrs M'Cotton when she got home. A battered old taxi, fetched by Peter from the village, drew up at the gate of the field, and their equipment, ' camping, for the use of,' was trundled down to the left luggage office at the station. After that the taxi returned to the field gate to pick up four passengers en route for the five-mile-away hotel, both Sarah and her daughter being ashamed of the vehicle's shabbiness and fearful for the impression it would cause on their prospective fellow guests. But they need not have worried, for their arrival was not observed. When they had been shown their allotted rooms, mother and daughter got in each other's way in their anxiety to unpack, undress, wash and redress in a very small space. In the middle of the muddle Willie's voice was heard at the other side of the door :

' Heh, Serah, Ah cannae find ma new pullover ! '

Sarah opened the door and pulled her husband inside quickly, saying, as she closed the door, ' Willie, for goodness sake don't come wandering in and out of this bedroom as if we were in a room and kitchen. Anybody might see you and you without your jacket on and your braces hanging loose.'

The man was indignant, demanding to know what was wrong with coming into his wife's room.

' Clear out, Dad ! ' ordered Maisie from the dressing-table. ' Mother and I are on our own for this week-end. And anyway, you can't wear a pullover at dinner.'

' Whit-wey no' ? Ah've been daein' it fur years.'

' Well, you're in a hotel now, and you've got to do as other folk do. As a matter of fact you should've had dinner tails for a hotel like this.'

' Dinner tails ! Help ma boab—whit next ! ' He opened the door and disappeared along the corridor, yelling uninhibitedly, ' Hey, Peter—did ye hear that ! We shoulda brung wur dinner tails ! '

' Shsh ! ' hissed his wife after him. ' Don't bawl like that ! '

Closing the door she turned to her daughter for sympathy, but instead of sympathising, Maisie said she thought it was a mistake to have brought her father to a swell hotel like this. ' He'll worry the life out of you,' she warned.

' I know, but I've been trying to train him all week—table manners and that kind of thing.'

' Why didn't you go to one of the hotels in Drumforber ? There's none of them half so posh as this.'

' Because I wanted a fresh start somewhere. I wanted to be in a place that didn't know we'd been pigging along in a tent for a fortnight.' She preened herself in front of the only mirror in the room. ' How's my new frock at the back ? '

Maisie poked and pulled at the garment in question, pronounced it ' all right,' and added, ' I say, what about a dash of lipstick to give you some courage ? '

' Me ? Courage ? I'm not frightened. As long as a person acts natural they don't need to be frightened for any lord or lady.'

' Cheer up,' said Maisie. ' Maybe there won't be any lords or ladies.'

' Oh, but I hope there are ! It'll be something else to blow about to Mrs M'Cotton. Here—I must go and see how that pair are getting on next door. D'you think I could sneak along without anybody seeing me ? '

' Leave them to themselves, Mother. You're like a clocking hen with them.'

' Oh, Maisie—what a thing to say to your mother ! '

Nevertheless she took the girl's advice and restrained herself for five minutes ; then the pair of them joined the two men en route for the lounge. At the door Sarah turned on her husband.

' Now, look here, Willie, for goodness sake try and behave yourself with some—some dignity. After all, people only accept you at your face value, and if you talk like a—like a Glesca keelie, they'll think that's all you are.'

' Ach ay. Jist you watch me ! ' was the retort ; then, lifting his chin, he added throatily, ' Good evening, Lord Nose-hooh. And how many deahs did yaw shoot to-dye ? '

'Deer, Dad!' said Maisie with the maddening rightness of the teacher.

'My, ye're awful affectionate a' of a sudden,' said Willie, reverting to his natural voice and not misunderstanding her in the least. 'Are ye wantin' the len' o' money?'

At that Peter created a distraction by complaining that his collar was too tight for him; he had discovered the discrepancy on seeing a very pretty waitress pass by their little group. But his mother dismissed his discomfort by telling him he looked very smart. Trying unsuccessfully to see her reflection in the bulbous glass of a butler's mirror, she demanded of Maisie if her hair was all right.

'It's fine,' said Maisie, 'but I wish you'd put on a spot of lipstick. It would take away from the high colour you've got with all this excitement.'

'If you wid take some o' that muck aff *your* face,' began Willie, when his wife interrupted him. She, too, was becoming conscious of the pretty waitress who was passing once again.

'Let's get into the lounge!' she ordered. 'We don't want the hotel people to think we're frightened.'

'Ah'm sure Ah'm no' feart!' boasted Willie.

'That's just it! I wish you were. Well, come on. Open the door, Peter. And Maisie—if I make a mistake in grammar will you please not correct me in front of people?'

'Okay,' said Maisie resignedly.

Halting Peter's hand on the door-knob, Willie whispered, 'Will there be somebody inside tae introduce us?'

'Of course not!' Maisie made the most of the sibilant.

'Then hoo'll we know whit tae cry them?'

'Shsh.' The sibilant came this time from Sarah. 'There's that maid away past again. I'm sure she's laughing at us. Open the door, Peter.' But the maid, safely hidden in the shadows, was out of sight again, and Sarah herself stayed the lad's hand. 'Just a minute. Maisie—supposing a lady—you know, a title and all that—should speak to me. Do I say "Your Ladyship" or "*my* Lady"?'

'Neither, Mother. Don't say anything.'

31

'Whi'd ye say if it's a duke?' whispered Willie.

'Your Grace!' said Peter.

'Peter, don't be irreverent!' The injunction came, as usual, from Sarah, who added, 'Now mind, Willie, don't tell a soul we've just been camping.'

'Ach you. Open the door, Peter.'

The door was opened, and they filed in. For a moment they could hardly believe the evidence of their own eyes; it was Sarah who found her voice first: 'Goodness, there's nobody here! Oh, what a relief! I was all keyed-up. Oh, isn't this lovely, Maisie?'

Still at the stage of mock-sophistication, Maisie refused to be enthusiastic; she admitted, however, that the room was quite nice, and that she rather admired the effect of pale green and silver carried out in the drapings and wallpaper. This in turn alarmed her father, who warned her not to be getting big ideas into her head about their 'pawrlur' as he called it. The quietness of the room, however, filled him with his own brand of content, and he sat down in one of the big chairs, saying that he had forgotten that chairs could be so soft. 'D'ye think,' he muttered impishly in his wife's direction, 'Ah could smoke ma pipe in a swell place like this?'

'No!' Sarah almost shouted the syllable. 'There's a smoke-room downstairs.' Turning to Maisie she went on, 'D'you not think it's awful queer there's no other guests?'

'Maybe they're all out in their cars.'

'Yes.' Peter was delighted with his own humour. 'Huntin', shootin' and fishin'.'

But his mother had not heard the phrase before. 'Now, don't *you* start talking like your father!' she commanded.

Peter started in on self-justification, but Maisie cut into his speech with, 'Mother—look how that long narrow mirror gives an effect of height to the room.'

'So it does,' answered Sarah, peering at the article in question. 'D'you know I could enjoy myself fine here if only . . . ehm— d'you think I could risk taking off my new slippers? They're terribly tight.'

'Whit wey did ye no' bring yer Mother's hand-knitted slippers, Maisie?'

'It didn't occur to me,' she answered truthfully.

From the window overlooking the river Peter turned eagerly. 'I say, Maisie, dinner won't be for half an hour yet. What about going out for a walk?'

'Well, take Susan wi' ye,' put in Willie, still smouldering under the heat of his grievance that dogs were not allowed in public rooms. 'Puir wee sowl. She'll be lonely doon in that cauld kennel.'

'Okay.' Maisie included her father and brother in her willingness to be obliging, and the two young folk left the room. Too late Sarah remembered she might have asked Maisie to bring her knitting to her; Willie, not quite appreciating the luxury of his wife's undiluted company in such august surroundings, offered to fetch the knitting himself.

'No, don't bother. I'll just take one of these magazines in my hand. And if anybody comes in I'll look as if I'm reading.' At that moment a shadow appeared on the glass panel of the door, and she reached out hurriedly for the first magazine on the pile. 'Somebody's coming!' she whispered. 'Now mind—speak proper.'

The door opened and a burly man came in, dressed in what Sarah recognised as 'sporty tweeds,' but she was horrified to see the number and extent of the leather patches adorning it. Surely, if the man was so poor that he had to wear patched clothes, he must feel very out-of-place in this swell hotel? She watched, in the reflection of a dark picture, the man as he went silently to the window and gazed out. There was something about him, she decided, that she didn't like. He might at least have said 'good afternoon' to them. Suddenly she had to give all her attention to the magazine in her hand, for the man was coming towards her. No, he was stopping at the pile of magazines she had so recently raided. He was looking and looking at them. Was he looking for the one she had in her hand? The silence was unnerving her. In desperation she burst out :

33

'Is it this magazine you're looking for?' She held it towards the man.

But he hardly glanced at it. He turned towards the window again with a cool 'No thanks' spoken in a husky voice that made a chord of reminiscence throb in Willie's brain. It was his turn to watch the man. Suddenly, to his wife's humiliation, he slapped his knee and roared:

'Help ma boab—if it's no' Geordie M'Canvas! Hoo are ye, Geordie!'

'Willie McFlannel!' The answer came in such a raucous voice that Sarah winced. 'By a' that's wonderfu'! Fancy seein' you here! Hoo are ye, man!'

As the two men shook hands lustily Willie declared he could hardly believe his eyes—after all those years—was it twenty?

The stranger admitted that it had indeed been as long as that since they had last met. 'Is this the wife?' he asked, with what looked to Sarah like a leer in her direction.

'Ay—here, Serah, this is Geordie M'Canvas. Him an' me used tae run wi' milk when we were boys.' Sarah's intention was merely to bow in the general direction of her husband's ex-colleague, but her hand was grasped just as lustily as Willie's had been, her cold 'How d'you do' being drowned by 'Whit are ye daein' here, Geordie?'

'Oh, holidays. Man, Ah wid nevera knew ye if ye hadnae'a spoke the now. Ye're lookin' well.'

'Ay,' said Willie, forgetful of his wife's instructions as usual, 'we've jist been steyin' in a tent fur a fortnight. Ye're kinna weel-fed lookin' yersel'!'

With a cheerful wheeze, Mr M'Canvas slapped his convex waistline. 'Oh, ye mean ma bow-windae? Ay—Ah'm ay at hame at meal-time. Here—hoo's yer brither Mattha gettin' on?'

'Ach, he's jist the same auld caird. Aye tryin' fur tae sell ye somethin'.'

'Is 'e still bothered wi's corns?'

'Ah'll say 'e is!'

The introduction of her disreputable brother-in-law's name was too much for Sarah's powers of endurance; she got up and walked with as much dignity as her pinching slippers would allow towards the door. Her husband demanded to know where she was going.

'Upstairs,' she replied, her nose in the air ; 'to change my slippers.'

As the door opened and closed the two men looked at each other sympathetically.

'Uh-huh !' said Mr M'Canvas, ' Ah'm feart ye've said somethin' tae annoy the wife, Willie !'

'Ach, it'll 've been me talkin' aboot oor Mattha's corns that's minded 'er aboot 'er new slippers pinchin' hurs.'

They were neither of them of the type to worry unduly about anything for long ; they moved towards the most comfortable chairs simultaneously.

'Whit've ye been daein' wi' yersel' a' these years ?' asked the newcomer.

'Och, cawin' awa', Geordie. Cawin' awa'.'

'Still in the same shipyaird ?'

'Ay. Oh ay.'

'Hiv they no' made ye managin' director yet ?'

'Naw. Jist foreman. Whit aboot yersel' ?'

'Oh, no' bad,' said Mr M'Canvas complacently and in complete disregard of his patched sportswear. 'In fac', Ah sometimes say tae the wife, " Whit wid wur Springburn friends think if they saw us noo ? " But—ehm—the wife disnae like tae be reminded aboot Springburn.'

Willie flashed a look of sympathy towards his old companion, but in a moment his memory caused him to burst out laughing. 'Man—Ah often hae a bit smile tae masel' when Ah mind o' thae auld days. D'ye mind thon frosty day when the baith o' us fell an' skailt hauf the mulk oota wur cans an' we tried tae make it up wi' pipe-cley water ?'

Once again the wheezy laugh rang out. 'Ah'd forgotten that, man !'

'Whit line are ye in ?' asked Willie.

'Oh, steel, man. Steel. Ay. Ah've done no' bad. Cleared three thousand last year.'

'Three thuth-thousan'? Jeengs, whitna lota Income Tax ye musta had tae pey on that.'

'Ach, that was whit was left efter Ah peyed ma Income Tax. Wait till ye see the new car Ah got last week. The wife's away oot in it the noo. Have you got a car?'

'Me? Naw. Whaur are ye steyin' nooadays?'

'Doon in Kilmacolm. Man—it takes a terrible livin' up tae, but the wife manages it fine. Better nor me. She'd hae a fit if the folk roon-aboot wis tae get tae know Ah used tae cairry mulk.'

'Ah'll never let dab,' promised Willie.

'Have ye been daein' much fishin' since ye arrived?'

'Me? Ah don't fish.' The very idea was utterly alien to Willie, but he added politely, 'Dae you?'

'Sure! Ye should see the whopper Ah got this mornin'. Ah handed it in tae the cook at the hotel here. Ah tell ye whit —come on doon till we see if she's touched it yet.'

Any doubts Willie might have entertained that his old friend was pulling his leg on the subject of fishing were now removed. Getting to his feet he admitted he knew nothing whatever about fish except that aspect of the subject which he gleaned from surreptitious visits to fish-and-chip shops. 'D'ye mind,' he gurgled reminiscently, 'when we caught the eel thon day we wis fishin' fur baggies in the canawl?'

'Fine Ah mind it!' Mr M'Canvas opened the door. 'Come on doon the stair an' Ah'll show ye ma fishin' tackle when we're at it.'

In the doorway Willie almost collided with an elegant lady who had suddenly turned the corner. Seeing her, Mr M'Canvas mentally drew himself together and, with a marked improvement in his speech, he said:

'Oh, Willie. This is my wife. Alice, this is an old friend of mine—Mr McFlannel.'

The elegant lady was more successful than Sarah had been in ignoring the outstretched hand. 'How do you do,' she said aloofly.

But Willie was undaunted. His happiness at the renewal

of an old acquaintance bubbled up, and, losing touch with all his promises, he blurted out affably :

'Hoo'ye. You'll no mind o' me, Missus. You wid be a wee lassie wi' a dolly when Geordie an' me wis cairryin' mulk.'

'I beg your pardon !' said the lady with more indignation than apology.

Willie, however, fastened on the non-existent apology. 'Oh, it's a'right. Ah didnae hear onythin'. Ah see ye've been guid tae yer man. That's some corporation he's got on him.'

Mrs M'Canvas looked at Willie from head to foot and her husband, knowing the devastation intended thereby, took Willie's arm, saying :

'Come on, Willie. What about seeing that fish ?'

'Well, jist as ye like. Cheeri-bye the noo, Missus. The wife'll be awful glad tae meet ye.'

The two men disappeared, leaving the woman to make her lady-like way towards one of the comfortable chairs. She was rummaging amongst the pile of magazines when the door opened once more ; Sarah, having changed her slippers, advanced with the purposeful intention of making a social conquest. Her speech was studiedly careful as she asked :

'Is it this magazine you're looking for ? I took it to my room just now by mistake.'

'So that's where it went ? I was reading the serial story in it.' She reached out her hand to take it, her head-to-foot glance taking in the value of Sarah's garments, visible and invisible, to the complete unawareness of the wearer, who sat down saying companionably :

'There don't seem to be many guests about this afternoon.'

'No. Of course the hotel has just been derequisitioned, and it's being opened up only gradually, so there are very few guests so far. Have you just arrived ?'

'Yes. Have you been here long ?'

'Only a week. We really intended going to the Continent —Switzerland this time—but my husband had to go to America on a business trip, and it rather upset our arrangements.'

Switzerland. America. Sarah was impressed, but tried to hide her reactions under a casual ' Oh ? '

' Are you from Glasgow ? ' asked Mrs M'Canvas.

' Yes. Oh yes.' The ice was getting thin ; Sarah skidded on to safer ground. ' Where do you come from ? '

' Kilmacolm. At least that's where we're living now. You know Kilmacolm ? '

Sarah searched her memory, playing for time. ' Well, I've passed through it in the train. But . . .' What she was about to say caused her grave self-disgust, but she carried on : ' I've heard my friend Mrs M'Cotton speak about a family called McSequin. Do you know them ? '

' I do indeed. Very nice people, they are. Very nice.' Mrs M'Canvas's tones were becoming warmer every breath she took. ' They've just bought the most gorgeous yacht. How long do you intend staying here ? '

' Oh, just for the week-end.'

' Surely you didn't come all the way from Glasgow just for the week-end ? '

Ah. Thin ice again. ' Nun-no. We've been in Drumforber for a fortnight.'

' Oh, Drumforber ? You would meet the McMarocains there then ? Exceptionally nice people ! Their youngest daughter is being presented at the next Court, you know.'

Sarah admitted with some truth that she did not know, adding that she was afraid she did not meet the family in question.

' But I don't know how you could have missed them ! Drumforber is such a small place—you soon get to know everybody of any importance.'

' Well, you see . . .' Sarah fumbled for the right words. ' We kept ourselves pretty much to ourselves.'

' And how right you were ! ' The magazine, forgotten, slipped to the floor as Mrs M'Canvas hitched her chair nearer to Sarah's. ' You never know the impossible people you sometimes have to meet in hotels. There was a perfectly dreadful man in here a few minutes ago.'

Her mind still full of the disgust with which Mr M'Canvas

had filled it, Sarah, in turn, hitched her chair slightly and said, ' Oh, did you see him, too ? Did you ever hear anybody speak like the way he did ? '

Mrs M'Canvas's mind occupied with Willie's social *gaucherie*, declared that she never did. ' I was disgusted ! ' she said. ' So vulgar ! '

' You would think that, in a hotel like this, they would be more careful about letting people like that in.'

Once again the chair was edged a little closer to Sarah. ' I feel one would be quite justified in complaining to the management about people of that type.'

Sarah agreed wholeheartedly, and the tête-a-tête might have gone on indefinitely had not Maisie opened the door and demanded to know where Peter had got to. The girl was looking particularly smart in a new outfit, and her mother yearned to introduce her to her new-found friend, but alas, the friend's name was as yet a mystery. Mrs M'Canvas, aware that the spell of intimacy might be difficult to renew after the interruption, got up and, excusing herself on the grounds that she had left her spectacles in her room, left mother and daughter together.

' Who's the dame ? ' asked Maisie irreverently when the door had closed.

' I don't know ; but I'm sure she's Lady Something-or-other. She lives in Kilmacolm.'

' It's a posh car she's got anyway. I saw her coming in while I was waiting downstairs for Peter.'

' She was terribly nice with me anyway. Wait till I tell Mrs M'Cotton about this.' A momentary qualm returned as she remembered the base uses to which she had put her unwilling friendship with that lady, but Maisie, knowing nothing of her mother's remorse, encouraged her to ' keep her tail up.'

This Sarah had every intention of doing, and said so. ' If only your father would keep his end up too ! D'you know, just after you went out, a perfectly awful man came in—the roughest Glesca keelie you could meet—and what do you think—your father and he suddenly discovered they used to run with milk together about fifty years ago. Isn't it awful ! '

' Huh,' grunted the girl. ' I'll bet Dad forgot all the lessons in English pronunciation he ever learned ! '

' Oh, of course—he was speaking the broadest Glasgow I've ever heard. It's right aggravating, so it is ! I don't know what that lady would think if she knew. If we could only get rid of that awful man, your father might be persuaded to hold his tongue.'

' Where is Dad anyway ? '

' Oh, he must've gone out with that man. I wish he'd stay out ! '

There was a bustle of conversation outside the door—Willie and his friend were returning ; Sarah's spirit cringed as the party advanced into the room.

' Oh, here's Maisie ! ' exclaimed Willie. ' Maisie—meet ma auld frien' Geordie M'Canvas.'

' How do you do,' said Maisie politely.

' How do you do,' said Mr M'Canvas with equal politeness and a courteous handshake which was in itself a tribute both to his wife's training and to his old friend's good-looking daughter.

' Him an' me used tae run wi' mulk thegither,' said Willie.

' Shsh ! ' implored the ex-milkboy. ' The wife might hear ye.'

At that moment Maisie caught sight of Peter bringing up the rear. ' Where did you get to ? ' she demanded.

' I went down to the kennels for Susan, and I met Dad and this gentleman measuring a fish.'

' Gentleman ! ' whispered Sarah derisively.

But that worthy, oblivious of the animosity being directed towards him, asked cheerfully if Mrs McFlannel had seen Mrs M'Canvas yet.

' No. I have not.' The answer was cold.

' Hur an' you wid get on like a hoose on fire.'

This Sarah interpreted as a near-insult ; she made no effort to disguise her feelings, and at last something of her attitude made itself apparent to the man for, turning to Willie, he whispered behind his hand that he was a sore trial to *his* wife.

' Jist like me wi' ma wife ? Eh, Serah ? '

But before Sarah could deny or affirm the suggestion, Mr M'Canvas suddenly left the room saying that he simply must fetch the wife. The closing of the door was the signal for Sarah to pounce on her husband.

'Willie ! What on earth had you to go and chum up with that man for ? He's a positive disgrace ! I haven't the slightest desire to know his wife.'

Then it was Maisie's turn, though in a different medium. 'Dad,' she said, 'I like the sweet thought of you and Mr M'Canvas " running " with milk. I've never seen a milk-boy running in my life.'

'That's because ye're no' up early enough in the mornin'.' Willie dealt with the easier problem first ; then turning to his wife he asked with mock innocence, ' D'ye no' like 'im, Serah ? '

' I think he's disgusting—and in a swell hotel like this ! How can we make a good impression on the other guests if you go and spoil things by making friends with a rough tyke like that ! '

' But, Serah, he's—— '

The woman cut off his partisan speech by saying, ' Now don't try to make excuses for him.' And then her speech in turn was cut off, for the door opened and Mr M'Canvas walked in, leading, almost dragging, his reluctant if elegant wife.

' Here she is, folks. Mrs McFlannel—meet Mrs M'Canvas ! '

For a moment the two women looked at each other in horror ; Mrs M'Canvas was the first to find her voice. Pointing her fore-finger to Willie she addressed Sarah :

' Are you that man's wife ? '

Nodding, tears not far off, but amusement glinting through, Sarah pointed to Mr M'Canvas and exclaimed, ' And—are you *that* man's wife ? '

The situation was pregnant with humour. Each member of the party succumbed to it—so much so that the gong sounding for high tea was almost drowned. But not quite.

' Cheers—the gong ! ' wheezed Mr M'Canvas, still laughing. ' Come on, folks. Ma stummuck thinks ma throat's cut.'

Once again the two women exchanged looks. There was, they each realised, a world of community in their problems.

41

CHAPTER 4

SARAH AT HAMPDEN

THE good weather lasted throughout the week-end ; it travelled to Glasgow with the family on the Monday, and by the following Saturday morning it still had not blazed away. They gulped their breakfasts, Peter gulping the football information from the morning paper at the same time.

' I say, Dad,' he mumbled through a mouthful of food, ' Colin's playing this afternoon.'

' Where ? Centre forward ? '

' Uhha.'

' See's the paper.'

' Just a minute till I see the team ! '

' Team ? Ah tellt ye afore, Peter—Queen's Park isnae a team —it's a dancin' class ! '

' Dad, the first time you said that I thought it was quite smart —now it stinks.'

' Peter ! ' exclaimed his mother, ' don't you talk like that to your father ! Ehm . . . is that your cousin Colin you're talking about ? '

' Yep. What about coming to Hampden to see him playing ? '

' What ! Me ! I would never demean myself by going to a football match.'

' Ye widnae demean yersel',' said Willie. ' There's lots o' weemin goes tae fitba' matches.'

' Huh—women, maybe, but not ladies.'

At that Maisie entered the conversation. ' Look out, Mother,' she said ; ' I'm going to the match.'

Drowning his wife's expressions of incredulity, Willie said, ' Guid fur you, Maisie. Whit team are you supportin'—Ah mean —whit side ? '

But before she could reply Peter had nipped in sarcastically with : ' Are you going on your own, or have you managed to get somebody to pay you in ? '

' You'd like to know, wouldn't you ! '

' Oh, Maisie,' wailed Sarah, ' I always thought it was only rough kind of sporty women that went to football matches.'

' Ah tell ye whit, Serah,' said Willie ; ' you go, an' we'll get ye a sate aside the bowler-hat brigade. An' in nae time ye'll be yellin' like the rest o' them, " Come away the Queen's. Don't let the nesty Rangahs beat you." '

' I wouldn't know one team from another,' confessed Sarah.

' Ye'd soon spot the Queen's,' commented Willie. ' They wear lace roon the foot o' their pants.'

' Willie ! Don't be vulgar ! '

' You haven't told us yet who you're going with, Maisie,' Peter reminded his sister.

As casually as she could, Maisie said that Jim was taking her ; that it was indeed the same Jim who, in his neat blue uniform of an Air Force pilot, had been entertained to tea some months before. Her father's disgust found expression.

' Ach—anither Queen's Park supporter. Serah, ye'll need tae come an' help me tae haud up the Ranger's end.'

' Oh, but,' the woman demurred, ' if I was going it would only be to see Colin. What team is he playing for ? '

Peter rushed in with adolescent enthusiasm to tell her he was playing for ' The Queen's.'

' The only thing is—I don't think I could stand on my feet for—well, how long does a football match last ? '

' An hour an' a hauf,' replied her husband. ' But ye could go tae the stand.'

' But that's what I'm saying—I couldn't stand all that time.'

' Ye'll get a sate in the stand ! '

That was different, though. She confessed she *would* like to see her sister's boy playing in an important match, and besides, if Maisie was going——

' Oh, but Mother,' protested Peter, ' you don't want to rush in on Maisie's little affair, do you ? Love's young dream and all that sort of thing.' He squirmed as a cushion came flying in his direction, and left hurriedly for his work, leaving his mother with the other two to make the arrangements for the family outing.

The afternoon sunshine—surprisingly strong for September—poured down on the great bowl that was Hampden Park. The McFlannel party, to Sarah's great content, was seated near the front ; she admired volubly the exceeding greenness of the grass at the centre of the bowl, adding, ' Somehow I never expected to see grass here.'

' Did ye expect it tae look like the Saut Waste ? ' demanded her husband, who was not feeling too comfortable on account of the carrying quality of her voice. His discomfort increased as Sarah remarked on all she saw, wanting to know where the men in bath chairs were being wheeled to. Willie was glad when Jim, Maisie's refined escort, took up the task of answering the queries and explained that there would soon be a line of chairs at the opposite stand ; they were wounded soldiers, he explained. Sarah's admiration of this piece of thoughtfulness on the part of the football authorities was broken into by her husband's yell :

' Heh, Serah, look who's sittin' behind us ! Geordie M'Canvas. Hoo'ye, Geordie ! '

' Hullo, Willie ! ' Mr M'Canvas's tones were even more far-reaching than Sarah's, but Willie could not be expected to notice that. ' Fancy seein' you here ! And the wife ! How are ye, Mrs McFlannel ? '

' Good afternoon, Mr M'Canvas,' said Sarah ; then, clutching at a straw of respectability, she added, ' Is Mrs M'Canvas with you ? '

' No fear ! ' The answer plunged her into the depths of gloom. ' Catch the wife comin' to a football match ! She's too genteel ! ' His horse-like laugh was heard by half the occupants of the grand stand. As the man turned to greet Willie more particularly, Sarah whispered :

' Maisie, did you hear that nasty crack ? '

' No, Mother. What was it ? '

'Mr M'Canvas says his wife is too genteel to come to a football match. I wish I'd never come.'

'Don't worry, Mother. Look—there's lots of ladies here.'

Sarah looked and agreed that some of them were quite well
dressed. Only half comforted she turned back to Mr M'Canvas
again who was asking her which team she was supporting.

'Oh, I'm not supporting any team. My nephew Colin's
playing today, and I just came to see him.'

'She disnae even know whit side 'e's playin' fur, Geordie,'
explained Willie.

Once again the horse laugh assailed the ears of those near and
far. 'Ye'll easy pick him out, Mrs McFlannel. Centre forward.
Ye'll be awful proud if ye see 'im gettin' a goal—eh?'

'She'll need tae be lucky as well as prood,' put in Willie.
'The Rangers'll win four-nothing.'

Mr M'Canvas's generous attitude towards the Queen's Park
team was unappreciated by Sarah, for his remark that he would
make it three-nothing conveyed no meaning to her. 'Hallo,
Maisie,' continued the gentleman, 'I never noticed you were here
an' all. How are ye?'

'Good afternoon,' shouted Maisie. 'I don't think you've
met Jim, have you?' She poked Jim, who wheeled round
for the introduction which he acknowledged in his usual
refined accents—accents that called forth the observation from
Mr M'Canvas that Jim would be supporting the Queen's.

'Yes, of course,' said Jim. 'However did you know?'

'Oh, maybe it's the way ye speak. . . . Oh, you're here
an' all, Peter!' The two waved to each other. 'The Clan
McFlannel's oot in full force the day—eh?'

'You're telling me!' Peter's smile vanished as he caught
sight of his mother's more than usually worried expression. He
asked her what was wrong now.

'It's all these men with the stretchers.' She pointed. 'They're
not expecting a bad accident, are they?'

Willie answered before Peter had time to do so: 'Thae's
fur cairryin' aff the bits o' the referee efter he's been hung, drawn
an' quartered.'

45

'Does the referee always get hurt?' she asked timorously.

'Shsh, wumman. Fur the luva mike don't let folk hear ye askin' sichna daft question or Ah'll be sorry Ah've brung ye.'

'What are the policemen for?'

'Shsh. There ye go again. Folk are laughin' at ye.'

Sarah examined the faces of the crowd. 'I don't see anybody laughing.' Then, as though to bolster up her flagging courage, she turned to Maisie, saying, 'Are you not amazed at the number of well-dressed women here?'

Willie overheard the remark. 'Whit did ye expec'?' he demanded. 'Shawlies an' ragwifes?'

At that moment there was a craning of necks; Sarah saw that interest was concentrated on some figures that were running on to the park beneath her. 'Oh, Peter,' she cried, 'is that Colin now?'

'No, that's the ball boys.'

'What are they for? Running messages?'

This time it was Peter who felt ashamed. 'Shsh, Mother,' he whispered. 'When the ball is kicked beyond the grass, these boys run after it and throw it back.'

'Oh, I see,' she answered, not whispering. 'They're sort of serving their apprenticeship, like?'

'Haud yer tongue, Serah,' growled Willie. 'Folk can hear ye. Oh, look—they're comin' oot.'

When the cheering had died down Sarah was heard to complain that they all looked the same, and which was Colin?

'Shsh! Colin's no' there!' Willie glanced furtively at his neighbours. 'That's a team—Colin's playin' fur Queen's Park.'

M'Canvas, sitting behind, saw the furtive look and made a noble gesture. Bending forward he whispered, 'Willie, will I ask this chap next me to change places with ye? You could come up here beside me an' nobody would know the wife was along wi' ye.'

But Willie, with equal nobility, declined the offer, saying he would be better to remain where he was so that he could, in the event of the worst coming to the worst, clout her over the jaw if she refused to hold her tongue.

46

Sarah, having missed the whispered conversation, found another worry to add to her repertoire : ' Goodness, what a lot of people are here ! How on earth are we going to get home again ? ' It might have been accident, or it might have been design ; at any rate she turned her head so that what she was about to say could be heard still more distinctly in the row behind her. ' All the cars and buses will be packed.'

M'Canvas's display of nobility was not yet over. ' Don't let that worry ye, Mrs McFlannel,' he roared. ' I've got my car here, and I'll give ye a lift. Bags o' room.'

Sarah tried not to show too much elation at the success of her ruse ; she admitted that it was real kind of Mr M'Canvas.

' Ay,' observed Willie ; ' a hurl in a motor caur disnae come your road every day, Serah.'

But once again Sarah's thoughts were wandering. The Rangers team were loosening their muscles by kicking the ball to one another. ' Oh look ! ' she cried. ' They've started to play and Colin's not here yet.' When the matter had been explained to her she allowed her eyes to wander again ; this time it was a hat, whose wearer had just entered the stand, which attracted her attention. She pointed it out to Maisie, who suggested the hat in question looked like the Leaning Tower of Pisa. The discussion lasted until Willie stopped it with his cry :

' Aw, Geordie, wid ye listen tae that ! Ah bring them tae a fitba' match an' they talk aboot hats.'

But Peter was ready with a distraction. ' Look, Dad,' he exclaimed, ' is thon not awful like Woodburn instead of Young ? '

It was Sarah who answered : ' I don't know how you can tell one from another. They all look the same to me.'

' You should be able to know them by their position, Mother. Look, thon's the goalkeeper—Brown.'

' But they keep running about all the time ! Why isn't Colin's team coming out ? '

' Because they're feart ! ' interposed Willie.

The raucous laugh burst forth behind them again. ' They'll be gettin' a wee cuppie tea to give them some spunk—eh, Willie?'

Vociferous cheering broke out at that moment. 'Here they come !' Maisie and Peter joined in the din. 'Come away the Queen's,' simpered Jim, with a polite clapping of his hands. 'Where's Colin ? Where's Colin ?' Even Sarah had to add to the shouting.

'Thonder !' yelled Willie, inadvertently adding to the tumult of welcome to his opponents. 'Look—bendin' doon.'

Right enough, thought Sarah, that's awful like Colin, but why was he bending ? To hitch up his socks ?

In answer to her unspoken question, Willie bawled, 'He's tryin' tae hide 'is blushes at bein' seen wi' Queen's Park. He could haud up 'is heid if he wis wi' a team like the Rangers.'

'Oh, he's looking over this way,' screamed Sarah in delight. 'D'you think he would see me if I waved my hand to him ?'

'He widnae see ye even if ye wis tae wave yer feet !'

Sarah turned to her daughter. 'Here,' she said, 'I never knew before that Colin had had rickets. Just look at his legs.'

Maisie looked and agreed that her cousin's shins were not showing a very noble outline, but as all the others seemed to be similarly rickety, she said frankly that she had never seen such a bunch of shauchly wee n'yaffs.

'Pipe down, you two,' roared Peter. 'They've all got shin-guards inside their stockings.'

'Why ?' asked his mother.

'In case they get kicked.'

Sarah was horror-struck. 'But surely they don't kick one another, do they ?'

'Naw,' snapped Willie. 'It's jist the bad Rangers boys that kick the nice Queen's Park lassies.' There was a hint of sneering in his tones that Sarah could not fail to notice, yet she asked :

'Then why are the Rangers wearing things down their legs too ?' But before there was time to answer that one she was caught up on another hook. 'Oh, look at them shaking hands. I'd 've thought they'd 've been introduced before they came on to the park.'

It was a subject upon which the genteel Jim could be relied on to be a specialist. 'It's a formehlity, Mrs McFlehnnel. The opposing ceptains always shake hends before a game. Look, they're tossing.'

Sarah kept quiet for a little, while her men-folk discussed details about the position of the sun in the sky, the wind and other natural phenomena as they related to the game of foot-ball; but soon she was showing once more the extent of her curiosity.

' Is that the referee with the yellow jersey ? What lovely fair hair he's got ! '

' Naw.' There was a hint of disgust in Willie's voice as he answered, ' That's Broon—the Rangers' goalie. Thon's the referee wi' the khaki jaiket on.'

Bewildered, Sarah scanned the field for the appropriate sartorial answer to her husband's description. Then, ' Where's Colin now ? ' she cried. ' The way they keep running about fair confuses me.' She winced on an intake of breath. ' Oh, did you see the way that man got hit on the head with the ball. Such a big ball too ! That must've been sore ! '

' Aw, Serah, fur peety's sake shut yer trap.'

Suddenly her ear-drums were assailed from behind. In his excitement the ex-milkboy was gripping both her shoulders and yelling, ' Offside, ya stumer ! Offside, there ! '

Willie, too, was on his feet. The incident had escaped him, but loyalty to his friend made him yell in unison, ' Offside ! '

' Maisie,' said Sarah, ' what does offside mean ? '

' Search me.' The girl turned to her companion : ' Jim, what does offside mean ? '

' Shsh ! ' Jim's manner had changed instantaneously. He had no interest in his girl friend—all his attention was given to the field of play. ' Don't speak so loud. I'll tell you after. Oh ! A foul ! '

' A foul ! ' yelled Peter in agreement.

' Away wi' ye,' snapped Willie, than whom there never was a more prejudiced partisan. ' He couldnae help it ! '

' Oh, look at thon man with the bald head, Maisie,' shouted Sarah. ' It's a wonder he doesn't wear a cap to hide it.'

' Serah, shut up ! ' The command could only come from an

indignant husband. 'You should wear a nose bag tae cover yer mooth.'

Maisie heard the remark and leaned sympathetically towards her mother. 'You and I don't seem to be terribly popular with our escorts at the moment. Jim's just snubbed me. I wish I'd never come—ugh, them and their old football.'

'Never mind, Maisie, it'll be fine getting taken home in Mr M'Canvas's car. I hope we pass the M'Cotton's house. Her that's always boasting about her swell friends and their cars !'

The conversation, despite the excited shouts all round, continued over a variety of subjects until Willie was moved to protest once more. 'Here, whit are you two gabbin' at ? Can ye no' watch the gehmm ? Look at Caskie—whitna wee needle !'

'He's a needle in a haystack as far as I'm concerned,' Sarah cold-shouldered her husband. 'Where's Colin now ? Can you see him, Maisie ?'

'No. I wish I'd brought the field-glasses. It's a lovely day, isn't it. It seems a shame to waste it at a football match.'

The two Queen's Park supporters suddenly broke into loud protests of ' Foul.'

'It wisnae a foul !' roared Willie. 'The referee sees mair than you dae. He's on the spot. Come on, Caskie, that's the wee dandy ! Thornton, noo ! Come on, Thornton !'

Sarah shook her husband's arm. 'Willie ! You tell me to keep quiet and you yell yourself like a bull ! Talk about folk laughing at *me* !'

Once again her shoulders were seized from behind, and once again her ear-drums were assailed with Mr M'Canvas's raucous commentary : 'Waddell's got it ! He's got it ! Shoot, man, shoot !' For a moment the grip on her shoulders was so excruciating that she wondered if a hurl in a motor car was sufficient to keep her from protesting. But the grip relaxed. 'Aw, he missed 'is chance there. Still an' a', he's a great player is Waddell.'

The game surged and sagged, the supporters gasped and grunted, yelled and wailed. In a little backwater of their own mother and daughter chatted contentedly. 'Maisie, I was just

thinking—supposing Mr M'Canvas suggested taking us down
to his house in Kilmacolm after this is over——'

'It would be a kind of long road for a short cut, would it
not?'

'Yes, but supposing——'

'Well?'

'I'm glad I've got on my best stockings. You're looking
quite tippy yourself.'

'But, Mother, I don't think there's the slightest chance——'

'Of course, I'm forgetting! You're here with Jim.'

'Oh, you can count him out. I'm in the huff with him. The
cheek of him—telling me to speak more quietly.'

'Shoot, man, *shoot*!' bawled M'Canvas.

'Come on, stop caperin',' bellowed Willie.

'Would you just listen to that!' said Sarah. 'And they'd
tell *us* to speak quiet! I don't know what Mrs M'Canvas'll
think of me, all the same, coming to a football match. It must
be a right grand house they live in in Kilmacolm with servants
and all. The worst of us going down there is that I'll be ashamed
to ask them back to our poky wee three-room-and-kitchen.'

'But, Mother, he hasn't asked us yet!'

'I'm hoping he will, though.'

At that, pandemonium broke out. All around hoarse voices
bawled something unintelligible. Sarah looked in bewilderment
at her dancing husband; why, she wondered, were Peter and
Jim taking it so quietly—whatever it was. 'What's all the noise
about, Maisie?'

'It'll be a goal, likely,' said the girl indifferently.

'Willie'—Sarah poked her husband's ribs with a corner of
her handbag—'was that a goal?'

'You bet it wis!'

'Was it Colin?'

'Don't be daft! It wis a goal fur the Rangers! There'll
be nae goals fur Queen's Park the day. They've just come here
tae see hoo fitba's played.'

'I'm sure I can't make head or tail of it. Maisie, can you
see Colin yet?'

'Ugh, I've lost interest in the whole show.'

'I wish,' said Sarah, 'they wouldn't run about so much. If Colin would just stand still——'

'Staun' still?' jeered Willie. 'He's that still, wumman, he'll fin' 'issel' stickin' up in George Square if he disnae watch oot.'

For a few minutes nothing exciting seemed to be happening. Then, for no reason at all, Jim and Peter flared up, shouting and stamping their feet, and Willie for once was quiet. Whatever the cause, there was pain on the face of Sarah's escort. Suddenly Maisie's escort began clapping his hands and saying, quite lustily, 'Goal!' But his enthusiasm seemed to reach an anticlimax when he added daintily, 'Jolly good show!'

'Was that another goal, Maisie?' asked Sarah.

'I'm sure I don't know,' answered Maisie huffily.

'Peter'—Sarah nudged her gesticulating son—'was that a goal? I wasn't looking.'

'Of course it was! Did you not see Colin getting it?'

'Colin?' All at once Sarah's polite inquiry turned to genuine excitement. 'I never saw a thing! Where is he? I can't make him out. Oh, I must give him a clap.' The uproar from the Queen's Park supporters had already died down, so Sarah's applause had an element of individuality about it. 'Isn't that nice,' she went on. 'Will he have his photo in the papers?'

'Maybe.' Peter's indifference was due to the fact that he was intent on the progress of the game, but his mother was not yet finished with the incident. 'Willie,' she said, 'why are you not clapping? That was Colin getting a goal! Are you not proud of him—your nephew?'

'Ach, don't scunner me.'

Once again the fruity laugh cackled at Sarah's ear. 'That's burst 'is coupon, Mrs McFlannel!'

'Naw, Ah've nae coupon, Geordie,' said Willie. 'Ah'm jist scunnert at bein' asked for tae clap ma haun's—as if Ah wis at a Bandyhope social. An' fur a Queen's Park goal, tae. Ach . . .'

'Will that be the game finished now, Maisie?' asked Sarah, not without hope.

'Oh dear, no ! There's another hour to go.'

'An hour ! I feel as if I've been here all day.' At that a wasp hovered menacingly near her face. She flapped at it in distress.

'Who are you cryin' hurray tae noo ? ' demanded Willie.

'I'm not crying hurray to anybody—I'm shooing away a wasp that's flying around. I hope I don't get stung.'

'Shoo it ontae the field, then, an' see if it'll waken up some o' thae men—staunin' aboot there as if they were sleepin'.'

'Heh, that wis a foul, was it no', Willie ? ' shouted M'Canvas.

Willie, although he had missed the last few seconds' play, nevertheless joined with his friend in yelling ' Foul ! '

'It wasn't a foul ! ' insisted Peter. 'It was Waddell that shoved him——'

'Away wi' ye ! ' roared M'Canvas. 'It wis your man. If you wid dicht yer nose maybe ye would see better.'

Sarah was horrified. ' Oh, Maisie, did you hear that ! The way Mr M'Canvas spoke to Peter. We'll never get a run to Kilmacolm now. Oh, poor Peter—he didn't deserve it.'

M'Canvas was getting hotter under the collar. ' That ball was never out ! Willie—did ye ever see sichna decision in yer life. That referee should buy a dug an' a tinny ! '

'The referee was quite right ! ' Peter flared round at the older man. ' The ball was well out ! He sees far more of the game than you do.'

'Getcher, man. I never seen a more bare-faced thing in ma life.'

'Pft ! You want the referee to be playing in your team ! '

Sarah nearly wept. ' Oh, Maisie,' she wailed, ' isn't that awful to hear Peter speaking like that to Mr M'Canvas. That settles our chances of getting to Kilmacolm. I feel like telling him to apologise. After all, Mr M'Canvas is an older man——'

'Better leave them alone, Mother.'

A lull in the game provided Jim with an opportunity to turn to Maisie and ask if she were quite comfortable.

'Don't speak to me,' was the retort. ' You might miss some of the game.'

53

The sarcasm could not be mistaken. 'Why—what's wrong ?
Are you not feeling well, dear ? '

'I'm *quite* well, thank you—and don't call me dear ! '

The swain was still obtuse. 'But, Maisie darling, can I get
you a drink of water ? '

'No—don't mind me. Just go on watching your old football
match.'

'But I don't understand, Maisie. . . .'

For a moment Sarah's gaze rested on the field of play. What
she saw made her wince. 'Oh, did you see that ! That must've
been sore when those two men hit the ball with their heads at
the same time.'

'Serah ! ' Willie looked murderous. 'Ye're making me
feel black affronted.'

'Well, manys a time I've been black affronted with you.'
She turned her back on her husband. 'Oh, Mr M'Canvas,
your garden'll be looking lovely just now, I'm sure.' But
at that moment the owner of the garden had eyes and ears
only for football. She prodded him. 'I was saying, Mr
M'Canvas——'

'Whit wis that, Mrs McFlannel ? ' The man brought his
attention away from the game with reluctance.

'Never heed 'er, Geordie,' snapped Willie. 'Imagine
bletherin' aboot gairdens at a fitba' match.'

M'Canvas did as he was told and ignored the woman. Dull-
ness settled down on the party, nothing occurring on the field
to cheer them. Jim bethought him of his lady friend. 'Maisie,'
he said, 'I wish you'd tell me what's the matter. Would you
like me to take you home ? '

'I'm quite all right, thank you.'

Without warning, Willie, his eyes glued to the field of play,
let out a yell of dismay. 'Aw, wid ye look at that ! ' Then,
waxing vituperative : 'Ah, ya *ham*—ye ! '

At that Sarah clapped her hand to her mouth in equal dismay.
'Maisie ! ' she moaned. 'Maisie—the ham.'

'What about ham, Mother ? ' asked the girl with only half
her attention.

'I've left the ham-and-mutton roll for tomorrow's dinner on the gas.' She got up. 'Oh, let me out of here. Quick.'

Annoyed with the sense of restlessness at his side, Willie demanded to know what was up, and why couldn't she watch the game.

'I'm going home. Where's my gloves?'

'But the gehm's no' right stertit yet!'

'I don't care. Oh dear-dear, the meat'll be ruined.'

Willie turned to his daughter for an explanation. 'Maisie, whit's goin' on here? Haverin' aboot meat at a fitba' match!' But before she could reply she was dragged to her feet by her urgent mother, and not all the pleadings of Jim nor the expostulations of the other menfolk could stay their rapid exit. It almost seemed as though the girl, not fully aware of the reason for their departure, was at the same time not unwilling to go.

As for the men, they looked at one another, a certain amount of strain and restraint leaving their faces. 'Ach, tae bleezes wi' theym,' said Willie. 'We'll get a chance tae enjoy wursels noo. Come on doon here aside us, Geordie.'

Mr M'Canvas took the necessary step to join his friends; was it imagination—or did the game really brighten up from that moment?

CHAPTER 5

IN THE PARK WITH IAN

THE following Saturday Willie and Sarah found themselves once more in the open air. This time it was because they had been begged by their elder daughter Polly to take charge of her little boy Ian for a few days. At seven years of age he was an unpleasant child, chiefly as the result of the erratic discipline his parents dealt out to him, and this afternoon his grandparents took him to the Botanic Gardens in an attempt to amuse him. When they had walked to the limit of their endurance, Willie and Sarah yearned towards a vacant seat on the skyline ; Ian, however, protested that he did not want to sit down.

' Come on, son,' wheedled Willie, ' ye can see the sheepie-mehs from thon seat. You take the dug on the lead an' Ah'll race ye tae it.'

' I don't want Susan ! I don't want to race you ! '

' Oh dear-dear,' wailed Sarah. ' It's me that's sorry I promised Polly to keep him.' Husband and wife exchanged looks of sympathetic exhaustion. ' See, Ian—would you not like to sit on thon nice seat and watch the sheepie-mehs having their dinner ? '

' There's no such things as sheepie-mehs,' was the contemptuous retort. ' It's sheeps.'

' All right. Come on and sit down and watch them.'

' Can I get throwing stones at them ? '

' Ye can nut ! ' The veto came from his grandfather. ' Sit doon an' we'll make Susan beg fur a sweetie ! '

Ian hung back from capitulation by demanding a sweetie for himself.

' You've had far too many sweeties, Ian,' said Sarah, reaching the seat and flopping down on it. ' They're bad for your teeth. You wouldn't like all your teeth to fall out, would you ? '

'I could get new teeth like my mummy and keep them in a tumbler at night.'

'Shsh. You shouldn't say things like that!'

Unwittingly the child sat down, fascinated by his grandfather's search for the poke of sweeties. The dog also was alert when it was finally produced, and the rustling of the paper indicated that it might be worth while adopting a begging posture. His mouth full of barley sugar, Ian surveyed the dog.

'Will Susan's teeth fall out 'cos she eats sweeties?' he asked.

'Maybe.'

'And will she get false teeth like you and Gran and Mummy?'

'Ah'm no' right sure, son,' answered Willie, attending to his dog. 'Ah never heard o' a dug wi' fa'se teeth ony mair nur Ah've heard o' a coo wi' a wudden leg.'

'If I threw a stone at yon sheep and it broke its leg, would it need to get a wooden leg?' The question had to be repeated, for Willie was by this time diverting himself with his dog's antics. 'You're not listening to me!' complained the child at length.

'Be quiet, Ian!' said Sarah. 'See—here's a lady coming to sit down beside us.'

When the newcomer had sat down Ian stared at her so much that even Willie could not but notice. 'Look, Ian,' he urged, 'look at Susan. She's beggin' tae ye. She's wantin' ye tae gi'e 'er a wee bit o' the sweetie ye're sookin'.'

'If I give her a sook will she give it back to me?'

The suggestion disgusted his grandmother, but before she had time to voice her feelings the child declared, 'Sure that lady's feet are awful big, Gran. Look!'

Sarah deposed the pointing finger with, 'Shsh. Here's a wee dog coming along with a tartan collar on.'

'I don't want to see a wee dog with a tartan collar on. I want to know why that lady's got such big feet with lumps at the side of them.'

The lady betook herself from the scene with as much speed as her bunion-infested feet would allow her, Sarah trying to improve on the occasion by insisting that she had gone to fetch the park policeman. But her threat carried little weight, for Ian's curiosity was greater than his fear. He sat swinging his feet, scraping his shoes against the gravel.

'Stop scliffin' yer toes like that!' ordered his grandfather. 'Ye're a restless tyke, so ye are.'

'What's a tyke, Granpa?'

Willie was saved the necessity of replying by the fact that an old man had appeared and was steering straight for their seat. The attention that had been paid to the absent lady's bunions was now focused on the newcomer's face as he sat down. To divert it Willie said, 'Look at Susan, Ian. See how good she is!'

'It's easy for a dog to be good.'

'Hoo d'ye make that oot?'

'A dog can't speak, so it doesn't get a thrashing for telling lies.'

'I'm sure you never got a thrashing in your life!' put in Sarah. 'You'd be easier to look after if you had.'

'Granpa, why is that old man's nose so red?'

'Shsh!'

Ian wriggled. 'Let me get down, Granpa. I want to ask the old man——'

'You'll stay where you are!' commanded Sarah with a shamefaced look in the old man's direction.

But Ian escaped. He reached within poking distance and said distinctly, 'Why is your nose red?'

'Whit wey am Ah no' dead?' The tones were indignant.

'Never heed 'im, mister,' said Willie soothingly.

'I said, why is your nose red?' repeated the child in spite of restraint.

'Ah am nut bow-legged,' insisted the slandered party.

'Ah'm awful sorry,' said Willie as loudly as he could. 'Ye'll hiv tae excuse the wean. He disnae ken ony better.'

'Whit's that ye say?' queried the deaf gentleman.

Willie bawled, 'Ah sayed, he disnae ken ony better.'

Mollified, the old man smiled. 'Oh ay. Ah'm a lot better. Ay. Ah've still a wee bit o' a hoast.' He cleared his throat by way of circumstantial evidence. 'But it's wearin' awa'. Oh, Ah had a bad time o't though. Ay. Since the montha July.

The eighteenth, it wis, Ah went intae the Infirmary—gravel in the kidney, ye ken. Ay. But they had tae operate on me efter a'—an' they got five stones ! Five ! Ah've got them wi' me in ma hanky.' Reaching into his coat pocket he brought out a handful of red cotton handkerchief which, on being prodded, was found to contain five small stones. Sarah was suitably disgusted with the demonstration, but not so Ian who wanted to play with them. But his grandmother's strictures were drowned by the voice of the old man : ' Ay. The doctor sayed it's a wonder Ah'm alive fur tae tell the tale.' Noting the child's intense interest in his treasures, he hid them once again in his pocket. ' Och, but Ah've suffered somethin' terrible. Somethin' terrible. Never oota trouble o' wan kind or anither. Ah had dip'theria when Ah wis six, then Ah had mumps an' measles an' muscular rheumatism. When Ah wis sixteen Ah had appendicitis. An' Ah've had pewmonia an' gastric flu an' jaundice an' lumbago an' sciatica. An' noo this. They were gey big stones, wur they no' ? '

' Ay. Oh ay.' Willie was the only one of the party who had the heart to answer the old man. ' Ye've been a guid frien' tae the doctors.'

' Ay—Ah've three dochters. A' mairrit. Yin o' them's oot in Canada. But ach, nane o' them's got ony time fur their auld faither. Ah'm a back number, ye ken. Ah could flyte on them tae Ah wis black in the face fur a' the guid it does. Hiv ye ony matches, mister ? '

' Naw, Ah'm feart Ah've come oot withoot them. Whit aboot you, Serah ? '

Insulted, Sarah snapped out that her husband knew quite well she didn't smoke. There must have been something in her facial expression which gave meaning to her mouthings, for the old man got up saying he would have to go home since he could not do without his smoke.

' Ta-ta,' called Willie after him. ' Tell yer doctor Ah'm sorry fur'm.'

' Oh, ye don't need tae be sorry. Ah didnae expec' ye tae hae ony matches—naebody has ony thae days. An' them newfangelt lighters are aye settin' fire tae ma whiskers. Well, so long.'

'So long.'

For a moment or two it seemed as though Ian were about to follow the fascinating hanky-wrapped stones. Sarah yanked him back on to the seat telling him not to be so restless.

'Ugh—it's not much fun coming to a park if you can't get being restless.'

Giving emphasis to his complaint, he swung his feet to and fro trying to see how near he could come to the dog beneath the seat without actually touching her. Then he whined that he was hungry.

'You can't be!' insisted his grandmother. 'It's no time since you had your dinner, and you had a slice of bread and jam before you came out.'

'Well, I'm thirsty. I want a drink. Can I not get a drink out of the duck pond?'

'You can not! It's nasty dirty water in there.'

'I want to see the ducks, then.'

'Ach well,' interposed Willie, 'fur peace sake, we'd better dauner alang tae the jeuks. It's jist roon the corner here.'

Sarah got reluctantly to her feet protesting that she did not believe in giving in to children, adding that more was being done for Ian than for any of their own four. To change the subject Willie asked the child if he would like to take Susan on the lead.

'Can I get taking her in beside the ducks?'

'No fear!'

'Why not?'

'Jist because.'

'Just because is a silly answer. Mummy's always saying it.'

He lingered behind for a moment or two until he was told not to dawdle. 'Keep in front,' urged Sarah. 'We haven't got eyes in the back of our heads.'

To which the child retorted, 'Oh, Gran, you'd look funny with eyes in the back of your head. Granpa could see all right, 'cos he's bald, but you would have to be always taking your hair out of the road. I would like an eye in the back of my head.

Why haven't we got one eye in front and another at the back?
Granpa—why haven't we got one eye in front and another at the
back?'

'Ah don't know, son. Ah'm no' yin o' thae modern painters.
Come on—we'll soon be at the jeuk pond.'

'Gran—do *you* know why we haven't got one eye at the
back and one at the front?' went on the persistent child.

'I do not. See—yonder's the ducks.'

'I don't want to see the ducks. I want to know why I
haven't got an eye at the front and another at the back——'

'You-want-you-want!' snapped Sarah almost hysterically.
'You'll do what your Granpa and I want for a change. Look at
that nice wee boy in front—walking along so good and quiet
beside his mammy. He's just a wee angel, so he is.'

'Granpa—do angels have one eye at the front and another at
the back? Granpa! Granpa, do angels——'

'Ah don't know, son,' said Willie wearily. 'Ah've never
seen an angel. Ah jist know they're supposed to have wings.'

'Oh, here's the ducks!' cried the child. 'They've got wings.
Are angels like ducks, Granpa?'

'Ach, never mind. Listen an' ye'll hear the jeuks sayin'
" quack-quack." '

'Have ducks got tongues, Granpa?'

'They must have or they couldnae say " quack-quack,"
could they?'

'Ducks have awful funny mouths, haven't they! Gran—
look at the funny mouths the ducks have.'

Glad that she was not being called upon to answer a question
Sarah responded kindly enough, 'Yes, I see them, Ian. Would
you not like to have kept a wee bit of your piece to put in the
ducks' mouths?'

'No,' he answered callously. Turning to his grandfather, he
asked, 'What's a duck's mouth made of? It's awful hard-
looking, isn't it!'

'Ay. It is that, son.'

'Well, what's it made of?'

'Ah couldnae tell ye. Ah've never been a jeuk masel'.'

'Oh, look at that duck turning itself upside down in the water! What's it doing that for, Gran?'

Sarah sighed. 'I don't know—unless it's getting something to eat at the bottom of the pond.'

'Why does it not fall to the bottom of the pond, Granpa?' Turning his back on his grandmother, he redirected his query, 'Why do ducks not fall to the bottom of the water?'

'Wait till you get hame an' ye can ask yer Uncle Peter or yer Auntie Maisie. Come on—there's mair jeuks over at the ither side.'

'Willie!' Sarah laid a restraining hand on her husband's arm. 'D'you not think it's about time we were getting home? All those questions——'

'Away wi' ye—we've hardly had time tae draw wur breath. Ian—look at thon jeuk. It's comin' oot the water tae see ye.'

'Oh, doesn't it walk funny! Why is it smiling, Granpa?'

Willie examined the duck's expression more closely. To be sure there was a look of mild amusement to be seen. He confessed ignorance as to the reason for the bird's smile, adding, 'Whi' d'ye think yersel', son?'

'Maybe it's smiling 'cos it sees us. Does a duck think we're funny, Granpa?'

'Ah widnae wonder.'

Sarah, fearful of further ornithological explorations, tugged at her grandson. 'Come on, Ian. You've seen the ducks long enough. What about going along for a wee minute to the Winter Gardens?'

'What's Winter Gardens?'

Said Willie: 'It's a place whaur they've got a' the plants an' trees an' flooers inside a big gless-hoose.'

Ian giggled, repeating the phrase 'gless-hoose.'

'There you are, Willie!' exclaimed Sarah. 'How often have I to tell you to speak proper in front of Ian? You'll have him as bad as yourself in no time. It's not a gless-hoose, Ian, It's a glass-house.'

'I think gless-hoose sounds nicer,' was Ian's opinion expressed with some obstinacy. Sarah was for skelping him there and then but Willie stopped her.

'Ach, lea'e the wean alane. We'll jist ca' the place the Winter Garden an' that'll please everybody. Wid ye like tae see inside the Winter Garden, son ? '

' Uhha.'

' Don't say " Uhha ",' expostulated the prim grandmother.

' You said it yourself, Gran. This morning. I heard you.'

This time it was Sarah's turn to change the subject ; she suggested an alternative objective, a move that was encouraged by the sight of someone going into the Winter Garden whom she had no desire to meet.

' Let's go along this path,' she urged. ' There's some more sheepie-mehs—ehm, sheep in that field. We can all sit down for a wee while on yon seat at the corner.' She led the way.

Amazingly, without protest, Ian followed, with Willie (nilly) at the rear. As they drew closer to the flock the child asked :

' Granpa—what are those funny things at the sides of the sheep's face ? '

' Them's horns, son.'

' What's horns for ? '

' Ah don't know—unless it's fur the men tae haud on tae when they're shearin' the sheep.'

' What's shearin' the sheep, Granpa ? '

' Aw, help ma boab ! ' exclaimed Willie, ' Ah'm no' a traivellin' dictionary. They shear the sheep so's tae get wool off them fur tae make clothes fur wee boys.'

' Is it sore ? '

' Is whit sore ? '

' When they take the wool off the sheep ? '

' Naw, it's no' sore. Is it sore when you get yer hair cut ? '

Ignoring the boomerang, the child demanded to know what sheep's horns were made of. Willie turned a pleading look on his wife.

' Aw here, Serah, could you no' take a turn at answerin' thae questions ? You're a couple o' years younger nor me—you should mind better whit ye were learnt at the school.'

'You carry on !' retorted Sarah. 'I'm enjoying myself. I'm waiting to hear what you'll say when he asks you why a sheep doesn't walk on two legs like himself.'

Willie groaned. 'Aw, fur ony favour, don't pit ideas intae 'is heid. Come on, son. . . .' He reached for the child's hand. 'Come on tae thon seat—there'll be bags o' room fur us as well as the wumman that's sittin' on it the noo. Look, Ian—Susan's watchin' the sheep.'

Suffering himself to be led in the desired direction, Ian pondered the problem before putting it into words :

'If Susan had a fight with a sheep, could Susan win ?'

'Never you mind !' interposed Sarah sitting down and pulling the child on to the hard bench beside her. 'You be a good boy now, and don't kneel on the seat. And keep your feet away from the lady's dress.'

The lady in question bent a kindly look on the child and assured the new arrivals that there was no need to worry—she had a grandson of her own about the same age. Not interested in the details that followed concerning the other child, Ian asked his grandfather if he might take Susan in beside the sheep.

'Naw,' said Willie with some firmness.

'Susan would maybe be frightened for such a big thing as a sheep,' put in Sarah as though to stem the flow of information coming from the newly met grandmother.

'Susan's not frightened for anything !' declared Ian. 'Neither's me ! Are you frightened for anything, Granpa ?'

'Ay. Whiles Ah'm feart for yer Gran.'

'Why ? Does Gran thrash you for telling lies ?'

'Sometimes.'

'Now, Willie !' protested Sarah, 'don't you be going and putting ideas into the child's head.'

'Your little boy speaks very nicely,' observed the strange lady. 'None of that horrible Glasgow accent.'

'Oh, his home's in Edinburgh,' said Sarah with some pride. 'His mother—she's our daughter—and father have a service flat there—out Morningside way.'

'Is that so?' exclaimed the lady. 'Fancy that! My daughter has a service flat too—near the Botanic Gardens.'

Sidetracking the unwanted data, Sarah suddenly gasped, 'Oh, where's Ian got to?'

'He's a'right,' said Willie calmly. 'He's in behind the seat here, playin' wi' Susan. Ah'm keepin' an eye on him.'

Thus relieved of grand-maternal duties, Sarah was forced to listen to and exchange information about the relative merits of the Morningside and Botanic Gardens districts in general and service flats in particular. They were deep in discussion when suddenly they became aware of an air of tension. A well-dressed gentleman had stopped in front of their seat; Willie had risen and was gaping at the new arrival.

'I say—it *is* McFlannel, isn't it?' said the stranger, holding out his hand.

Willie grasped it. 'My gosh, sir, it's yersel'! Ah hivnae seen ye fur aboot twenty year. Serah, this is ma auld colonel. Ah wis batman tae'm afore Ah wis drafted overseas.'

Sarah, not sure of the correct thing to do, shook hands and returned her attention to the lady, leaving Willie and his ex-colonel to carry on their own conversation.

'Ye're lookin' real well, sir,' said Willie.

'Thank you, McFlannel. You're looking pretty fit yourself. Is this your small son?'

In a moment of excitement, pleasure and grandfatherly weakness, Willie yielded up the dog's lead to the child as he disclaimed sole ownership. 'Naw-naw. That's my auldest lassie's wee boy —Ian. Are ye steyin' hereaboots noo, sir?'

'No—I'm in Glasgow only for a few days. You've changed a bit, McFlannel. Got a bit thin on top—what?'

'Ay, an' Ah'm no' near as skeigh as Ah used tae be, sir. D'ye mind thon night at Festubert?'

The colonel burst out laughing. 'Never shall I forget it, Mac. You said afterwards that you thought somebody had set fire to your shirt tail.'

The laughter grew louder as the two men revived each other's memories; the two women finding increasingly more in common got nearer to each other physically and mentally; Ian, taking advantage of the situation, slipped away unobserved.

'I suppose you would be in the Home Guard, Mac?' asked the colonel at length.

'Ay. Oh ay. No show withoot Punch, ye know, sir.'

'What rank did you hold?'

'Sergeant, fur ma sins, sir. Ah suppose you would be in it as well?'

'Yes-yes. Made me Zone Commander—for *my* sins. Jolly good show—what?'

'Ay. Ah whiles wish Ah could get slippin' oot tae the Home Guard some o' thae nights. It wis a rare excuse.'

Something of her husband's innuendo of furtiveness stole through to Sarah's consciousness; she bethought her of her grandson's capabilities in the same direction. She looked around, below, beyond. He was gone.

'Willie!' she shrieked. 'Where's Ian?'

'Is 'e no' wi' you?'

'No—I thought *you* were keeping an eye on him.'

Turning his back on the colonel, Willie too looked below the seat, but in the interests of truth we have to record that his search was for his dog rather than for his grandson. 'Whaur's Susan?' he roared. 'The wee deil!' he continued, referring to Ian. 'If ony hairm comes tae that dug . . .'

At the far end of the adjacent field there was a scurry of sheep with a child being dragged after them by a small excited dog. There was no time for valedictory ceremonials. The grand-parents raced for the spot, each of them eager to get there before the impending park ranger who was even now birling his whistle with all his might. Ian saw them coming, and would fain have changed his direction, but he was at the mercy of the dog. Wrath eventually made a three-point landing upon him, and chastened by the official's oratory, his grandfather's palm and his grand-mother's tears, he went home meekly. Going to bed that night, however, his natural thirst for information returned to him.

'Granpa,' he said, 'why does Gran always take a big breath when she looks at me?'

CHAPTER 6

A CHANGE FOR THE OLD MAN

WILLIE's brother Matthew (called Mattha for short) was by
reason of his passion for transacting business in all seasons never
a very welcome visitor at the McFlannel flat. Sarah regarded
his spasmodic appearances with grave suspicion. Willie, however, had a latent affection for his erring brother, and when he
went to the door one evening in response to the ringing of the
bell he exclaimed heartily enough :

' Aw, it's yersel', Mattha ! Come in—come in ! Hoo are
yer corns the day ? '

' Jist the same, Wullie,' was the mournful reply in Mattha's
chronically adenoidal tones. ' Whiles Ah don't know whether
Ah'm staunin' on ma heid or ma feet.'

' Ah never heard o' onybody haein' corns on their heid,'
observed Willie, as he conducted his visitor into the kitchen.
' Sit doon, man. Whit are ye up fur tae sell us the day ? '

Ignoring the question, Mattha sat down with an expression
of relief both facial and vocal ; he peered round the corner of
the scullery that was visible from his chair, whispering, ' Is Serah
no' in ? ' When Willie had assured him that she was out shopping, Mattha said that he would take off his boots.

' Jist as ye like,' said Willie. ' Ah think ma auld gas mask's
knockin' around somewhere.'

' Ye widnae make jokes aboot smelly feet, Wullie, if ye had
tae suffer like me.'

In silence Willie watched the removal of the boots ; a particularly loud yelp from Mattha, however, made him remark that
it was a wonder he didn't wear carpet slippers or elastic-sided
boots.

67

Making another grimace, Mattha said, ' Ah tell the wife she'll maybe see me on crutches yet.'

' Well, can ye no' go tae some hospital or ither ? Ah'm sure Ah've heard o' places fur foot an' mooth diseases.'

' There's naethin' wrang wi' ma mooth, but ! An' onywey hoo could Ah afford the money it wid cost tae go tae yin o' thae places ? Whit wi' the wife wantin' the room papered, an' us haein' the auld man tae look efter——'

' Oh, so ye're wantin' the len' o' five pound tae get yer corns pared ? '

' Ah never said Ah wis wantin' money ! ' Mattha flared up in indignation when he had recovered from the pain of taking off his second boot.

' Are ye sure yer buits isnae ower wee fur ye ? ' asked Willie.

' Naw, it's no' that. It's the leather that's aye sae hard. If Ah could get buits made o' soft stuff—like cloth——'

' That's whit Ah'm sayin'—carpet slippers is whit ye need. Ye could get ordinary soles nailed on. Ay—an' maybe roller skates forbye——'

Mattha caught the twinkle in his brother's eye. ' That's right —make a fool o' me ! ' he complained, then from peevishness the expression of his face changed to craftiness. ' Here—will Serah be long tae she's back ? ' he whispered.

' Ah'm no' right sure. How ? Are ye wantin' tae pit somethin' across me afore she comes ? '

' Well, d'ye see, it's like this——' began Mattha, when Willie interrupted him with :

' See here, Mattha—if it's money ye're efter, Ah've got nane. Serah jist gi'es me ma Setturday penny, so ye'd better haud off till she comes hame.'

With a glance that showed he knew his brother was guilty of some understatement of fact, Mattha went on to protest that the reason for his unexpected call had nothing to do with money.

' Right ye are,' conceded Willie. ' Oot wi't, then.'

' Well, d'ye see, Ah got the chance o' some rolls o' wallpaper.'

' Oh—an' ye want me tae gi'e ye a haun' tae hing it ? '

'Naw-naw. The wife an' me'll manage fine wursel's.'

'Ye're wantin' the len' o' ma paper-smoothin' brush, then?'

'Whit kinna thing's that?' queried the would-be paper-hanger.

Willie explained patiently, 'Efter ye've the paper on the wa', ye take a broad kinna brush wi' nae haun'le, an' smooth oot the blisters wi't.'

'Ach, when ye've suffered as much wi' corns on yer feet as me, ye don't bother much wi' blisters on yer haun's.'

'It's no' the blisters on yer haun's, man. It's the yins on the wallpaper.'

'Ach theym? Ah wis jist gonnae slabber the paste on tae the wa' an' sling up the paper an' then gi'e it anither slabber ower the tap wi' paste the same as the chaps dae when they're pittin' up bills on the sides o' bu'ldin's.'

'Away wi' ye!' exclaimed Willie from the profundity of his paper-hanging experience. 'That's no' the wey! See here——'

But Mattha was for none of his brother's advice. 'Ach, that wisnae whit brung me up,' he said without any subtlety in his attempt to change the subject. 'It wis the auld man.'

'Ye mean wur Uncle Donald?' asked Willie. 'Whit's up wi'm?'

'Well, d'ye see, it's like this. Wi' him sleepin' in the box-bed in the room, it's gonnae be kinna awkward——'

Willie laughed. 'Ay, it wid be a gey job if ye wis tae slabber some o' the paste on tae him. Could ye no' bung 'im ablow the bed tae the job's dune?'

'It's no' that. It's—well, d'ye see, wi' the hoose bein' in his name, like, an' us jist bidin' wi'm, we should by richts ask 'is consent fur tae get paperin' the room. But we're wantin' tae gi'e'm a surprise.'

For a moment Willie studied his brother's face, trying to discover the real motive that lay behind the apparent magnanimity towards his avuncular landlord. 'An' whaur div Ah come in?' he asked at length.

'Well,' Mattha took up the tale with alacrity, 'the wife

an' me thocht maybe you could invite the auld man up here fur a wee holiday. It wid be a chynge fur'm.'

'Ay?' Willie scratched his head. 'That wid be fur Serah tae say——'

At that moment a sound reached the kitchen which made Mattha make a hasty gesture towards his boots.

'Ach, dinna fash yersel',' said Willie. 'Ah'll jist open the windae,' and before Mattha had quite grasped the reason for Willie's hunger for fresh air, Sarah had opened the door. She took in the situation at a glance.

'Well, Mattha,' she said drily, 'I see you're quite at home. Are you sure you wouldn't like to take off your jacket as well?'

Unaware of the sarcasm, Mattha replied that it was real decent of her to suggest such home comforts, but he did not intend staying long enough to make the disrobing worth while. For a moment or two Sarah busied herself with the disposal of the contents of her shopping bag, then she asked how much Mattha had come for the loan of this time.

Willie got in first with, 'Nothin'. He jist came up fur tae ask me tae gi'e'm a haun' wi' paperin' 'is room.'

'Naw-naw,' protested Mattha. 'It wis aboot wur Uncle Donal', Willie! D'ye no' mind?'

While Willie nodded and Sarah sniffed, Mattha went on:

'Ye see, it's like this, Serah. The wife an' me wis gonnae gi'e the auld man a treat wi' paperin' 'is room, an' we thocht that, wi' the hoose bein' in his name an' a' that——'

'I see. You want us to lend you enough money to buy the wallpaper. Well, let me tell——'

'Naw-naw! We jist thocht if we could get him oot the road fur a coupla nights we could hae the job done an' nae bother tae him.'

'But where would the old man go?' asked Sarah.

'That's whit Ah came up fur tae see youse aboot,' said Mattha bravely. 'Ah wis wonderin' if maybe, well—ehm—could *you* no' gi'e'm a bed, Serah?'

Sarah nearly choked herself swallowing a shriek of amazement; Willie observed that Mattha wasn't asking much.

'Well,' retorted Mattha in an access of righteous indignation, 'he's as much your uncle as he is mine, Wullie. An' whit's mair —we've got the trachle o' lookin' efter'm a' the year roon. It's no' much tae ask ye fur—jist a coupla nights.'

'I won't have that dirty old man in my house!' said Sarah with emphasis.

Mattha embarked on a mission of cajolery. 'Aw, Serah,' he wheedled, 'think o' the treat it wid be fur the auld man. Youse've gotten sichna grand hoose wi' a bathroom an' a'.'

Willie's sense of family being strong, he took sides with his brother. 'Whit aboot pittin' 'im in Matt's room?' he suggested.

'I'm starting my Christmas cleaning extra early this year,' said Sarah, 'and I'll need Matt's room for keeping things in.'

'Ach but Serah,' continued the missionary, 'jist fur a coupla nights. He couldnae dae much hairm in a' that wee while.'

'I'm not so sure.'

Once again Willie's breeding was out. 'Come on, Serah. Efter a', as Mattha says, he's ma uncle as well as his. An' we've got the room. Whit's mair, it wid be somethin' fur the auld man tae mind on fur the rest o' 'is life.'

'That's right, Serah,' put in Mattha with some eagerness. 'It's no' much fun fur the auld man in a room-an'-kitchen. Nae place tae sit a' day but hing ower the kitchen fire, or maybe go ben the hoose fur a guid hing oot the windae. An' thae cauld days it's no' guid fur the auld chap. Although, mind ye, the wife aye sees tae it that he's gotten a cushion fur tae lean 'is elbows on. He widnae be much bother tae ye, Serah.'

'Well, he certainly wouldn't be allowed to hang out of *our* windows!' she retorted. 'The very idea.'

Mattha imagined he detected a softening in her adamant attitude. 'Then ye'll take 'im?' he said joyfully.

'I never said I would. I'd thought of having the McLeathers up some night.'

But the latter statement, instead of acting as a deterrent, put another argument into Mattha's lips. 'That wid be a real treat fur the auld man, Serah. He's that fond o' company.'

'Come on, Serah,' put in Willie. 'Jist fur a coupla nights.'

'It's not the nights that's worrying me, it's the days! I couldn't be doing with him hanging over the kitchen fire.'

'Light the pawrlur fire, then,' was Willie's suggestion, but it met with no approval except from Mattha who exclaimed that it was the very dab.

'Listen to me, the pair of you!' stormed Sarah. 'If you think I'll let that dirty old man sit in my parlour spitting into the fire——'

Before she had completed her threat, Mattha managed to nip in with, 'We'd gie'm 'is spittoon tae bring wi' 'im.'

The thought of a spittoon in the chaste surroundings of her sitting-room almost made Sarah physically sick; her momentary silence gave Mattha the chance to say:

'Ach, Serah, it wid be sichna nice chynge fur 'im. This braw hoose wi' a' the carpets an' everythin' polished that braw. Tae say nothin' o' yer grand bathroom. Ah wish ma wife could keep hur hoose as nice as this yin.'

Her sister-in-law's inefficiencies had long been a matter for self-preening on Sarah's part; there was nothing Mattha could have said more likely to please her. She said 'Well,' in a tentative kind of way that made her husband follow up his brother's advantage with:

'Ach ay, Serah. Ye'll be auld yersel' some o' thae days, an' maybe Peter an' Maisie'll be argy-bargyin' wi' yin anither aboot *your* spittoon.'

Which nearly lost the battle, for Sarah shrieked, 'Don't say spittoon to me again!'

'Ach,' said Mattha, 'he's jist kiddin' ye, Serah. Ah tell ye whit. The wife'll see that he washes 'is feet afore 'e comes, an' she'll gie'm a clean shift tae the buff forbye.'

While the woman hesitated, her husband pointed out that she should be glad she didn't have to put up with the old man all the time.

'You're tellin' me!' exclaimed Mattha with some feeling. 'The wife's near aboot dementit wi' 'im.' Then, realising he had perhaps done his cause damage by such frankness, he hurried to add, 'Ah mean tae say—it's no' that he's much bother—it's jist

—ehm—well—ach, he seems aye tae rub the wife the wrang wey.'

'And d'you not think he'll rub me the wrong way?' asked Sarah.

'Ach, Ah seem tae be openin' ma mooth an' pittin' ma fuit in it,' admitted Mattha.

'Ay—corns an' a',' commented Willie.

Mattha tried again. 'Whit Ah mean tae say is, Serah—the wife hasnae the patience wi' 'im that you wid hiv. An' think hoo gled youse wid be tae get the hoose tae yersel's efter he came hame tae us again.'

'Oh, well,' said Sarah, 'seeing it's just for two nights, I suppose we could stick it. And I daresay it *will* be a treat for the poor old man to get properly cooked food for once in a while instead of fish and chips every night in life.'

'Ay—an' jist think hoo divertit he'll be wi' yer bathroom,' went on Mattha.

'Diverted or no—he'll get a bath before he goes to bed,' said Sarah.

As Mattha bent to put on his boots, Willie slapped his wife playfully in the bye-going. 'Ye'll need tae watch an' no' droon the auld chap wi' kindness,' he commented.

A few days later all the preparations had been completed for the reception of the elderly visitor. There were fires both in the sitting-room and in Matt's bedroom; tea was set in the kitchen and Peter and Maisie had been instructed on their behaviour towards the old man, Peter's offer to take him to the ice rink meeting with little favour in his mother's eyes. Willie had gone to fetch him with surprising eagerness. The eagerness was still evident when he ushered Uncle Donald into the bright kitchen.

'Whaur'll Ah pit 'is bag?' shouted Willie from the hall, while the old man panted in the fireside chair.

'In Matt's room, of course,' answered Sarah, then, bending solicitously over the guest, she asked how he was feeling.

'Och, Ah cannae complain,' he admitted, 'but a' this jauntin' aboot'll be the daith o' me. Ah tellt Mattha an' Biddy Ah

73

wisnae needin' a holiday, but they sayed youse-yins wid be fair cut if Ah didnae come.'

'That's right,' said Sarah. 'Did you bring your slippers?'

'Me? Naw! Whit wid Ah be daein' wi' slippers? Stockin's holes is guid anuff fur me.' Then, since Peter seemed to be doing nothing, he added, 'Here, young fella—help me aff wi' ma jaiket.'

Knowing his mother's oft-expressed feelings on the subject of sartorial formality at the fireside, Peter said he was afraid she wouldn't approve. Sarah, however, was in a lenient mood.

'Oh, let him take it off if he wants to, Peter,' she said. Turning to the old man she added, 'We want you to feel at home, Uncle Donald.'

'That's real guid o' ye,' said he. 'Biddy said ye wid try fur tae make me act the gentleman. Help me aff wi' ma buits an' a', Peter.'

When Willie returned from the disposal of his uncle's luggage he found Maisie and Sarah busy with the final preparations of the tea, while Peter was kneeling to his task of taking off the visitor's boots.

'Whit's this?' demanded Willie. 'Have you got corns as well as oor Mattha, Uncle Donal'?'

'Naw—yer wife said Ah wis tae mak' masel' at hame,' answered the old man, tugging at his collar and tie and finally removing them both.

'Well,' said Willie in amazement, 'if you can get sittin' doon tae yer tea withoot yer jaiket an' yer buits an' yer collar an' tie, ye can get roon the wife better nur me. Ah wish ye'd tell me hoo ye dae it.'

Sarah took no notice of the remark; instead, she urged everyone to sit down around the table, reserving a special place near the fire for Uncle Donald, who looked surprised as he explained:

'Mattha's wife said ye'd make me eat at the jawbox.'

'She's a mean thing,' said Sarah, 'giving you a wrong impression of us altogether.' She helped him to sit down and propped a cushion behind him, but he was too intent on what lay before him to notice the luxuries in the rear.

'Yer knifes widnae need tae be shairp,' he commented, examining his portion of cutlery.

'Hoo that?' asked Willie.

'Well, ye wid cut the tablecloot wi' them. We aye jist use a newspaper an' ye can clean yer knife withoot worryin'.'

'In this house,' said Sarah pointedly, 'the cutlery's clean before you start.'

'What's for tea?' demanded Peter.

'Ham and egg—as a special treat for Uncle Donald.'

'Whit—ham an' egg?' spluttered the old man. 'Ah'm fur nane o't. Ah never eat meat twice in the one day. Ah had slice-sausage fur ma dinner.'

'But surely you'd like ham and egg.'

'Naw. Meat twice in the day's bad fur ma stummuck.'

'Well,' said Willie with regrettable inhospitality, 'gi'e me 'is ham an' let'm keep 'is egg.'

'Naw, Ah'm wantin' nane o' yer eggs eithers. Eggs is bad fur ma liver. Whit wey could ye no' 've had a fish supper the same as we aye hae at hame.'

'We thought you'd like a change,' said Sarah. 'Do you not get tired of fish and chips?'

'Whit wey wid Ah get tired o't? Gi'e me the things Ah'm used wi'.'

Sarah turned to her son. 'Peter,' she said, 'would you mind going out for a fish supper? I never thought——'

'Okay,' said Peter obligingly, 'but only on condition that it's me that gets Uncle Donald's portion of ham and egg and not Dad.'

Recognising the justice of the plea, Sarah set aside the unwanted portion, ignoring her husband's looks. 'Do you take sugar in your tea, Uncle Donald?'

'Ay. Twa spunfu's 'll dae.'

'Tutt-two?' stammered Sarah. 'Do you like your tea strong?'

The old man nodded, but when he saw the consistency of the

liquid that was being poured from the teapot he was driven to protest, ' Aw, but here—it's tea Ah want—no' that fushionless stuff ! It's a wonder that's got the strength tae stagger oot the pot. Ah like it stewed.'

' I'll need to make it specially for you,' said Sarah, but before she had risen from the table the visitor was expressing himself critically again. This time it was the coldness of the chair that had been brought from the sitting-room specially for him. While it was being warmed before the fire he continued :

' Ach, this is an awfu' cairry on. Ah'd 've been faur better tae've steyed at hame. Ah wisnae needin' nae holiday. Ah hope Ah don't get a chill in ma kidneys wi' sittin' on that cauld chair.'

Sarah's patience was wearing thin, but she managed to keep her real feelings out of her voice when she tried to comfort him, saying, ' I've had two hot-water bottles in your bed all day, Uncle Donald. And I've put an extra pair of blankets on too.'

' She's fair killin' ye wi' kindness,' said Willie, as though to emphasise the fact, but Uncle Donald remained unimpressed.

' Ay, but there's mair ways o' killin' a dug than chokin' it wi' butter.'

Not quite comprehending the significance of this contribution to the conversation, Sarah asked if oatcakes were acceptable.

' Nae oatcakes fur me,' said Uncle Donald frankly. ' They bring ma face oot in plooks. Plain breid's guid anuff fur me.'

' Right you are,' said Sarah. ' Here's the butter—real butter.'

' Ach, gi'e me maryjane. Ah've lost the taste fur butter.'

If Sarah said anything in reply to this it was lost in Maisie's announcement that the chair ought to be warm enough for occupation now. But even then things remained distasteful to Uncle Donald ; he observed a flutter of the window blind.

' Oh help ! ' he exclaimed. ' Is that yer windae open ? Nae wonder Ah wis cauld. Ah'll get ma daith o' pewmonia sittin' in a room wi' the windae open.'

While the window was being adjusted to suit him, the old man went on, ' Ah don't know hoo Ah wis sae daft as tae come here fur a holiday. It'll be nae holiday fur me if Ah've tae be laid up. See's me ma jaiket again.'

Maisie warmed the lining of the jacket before spreading it to receive its owner's arms. 'Ah think Ah'll jist sit doon at the fireside till Peter comes back wi' ma fish supper,' he said. 'Ah cannae be daein' wi' a' thae frills an' falderals like tablecloots an' dooble knifes. Saucers, forbye ! Ah like ma tea hot—Ah never tim it intae ma saucer.'

'Neither do we,' said Maisie, but her retort was unnoticed.

'This is a queer-like grate fur a kitchen.'

'Yes,' said Sarah, 'it's a new interior one. Isn't it nice !'

'Ach, Ah like tae get pittin' ma feet up on the hob—keeps them aff the draughts on the floor. There's nae hob here.'

'Ah'm thinkin',' said Willie in desperation, 'ye're gey ill tae please, Uncle Donal'.'

'Me ? Ill tae please ? Ah am nut ! Ah'm the easiest-goin' chap in the world—even although Ah say it masel' as shouldnae.' He paused, no doubt for agreement to be expressed, but none being forthcoming he found another item for criticism : 'Here —that's an awfu' high polish ye've got on yer waxcloth, Serah. Ah'll be feart tae walk on it. Plain boards is guid anuff fur me.'

'Well, I like to keep my house nice,' said Sarah with commendable, if forced, patience. 'I hope you'll enjoy being here, Uncle Donald. I want you to feel quite at home. You can go to bed whenever you want to. There's a fire in your room and Peter's fitted up a bedlight so's you can read in bed. And the water's piping hot for your bath.'

'Whit ? A bath, did ye say ? Whit wid Ah be daein' wi' a bath ? Ah'm no durty !'

'Ach ay,' said Willie soothingly, 'but wi' there no' bein' a bathroom in yer ain hoose, we thocht it wid be a change fur ye tae get a bath here.'

'Eh ? Me take a bath ? Ah'm never ower the door fur tae get durty. Mattha made me wash ma feet afore Ah came here —an' Ah wis fair fashed. Oh my, but this is terrible—whit between washin' ma feet an' cauld chairs an' open windaes—Ah'll never get ower it.'

Maisie took a hand in the mollifying process by telling him that Peter had come back. 'You'll feel better after you've had something to eat,' she added.

'Ah'm no' wantin' onything tae eat. Ah couldnae swally it. It's an awfu'-like thing tae come tae ma time o' life an' be driven f'ae pillar tae post like this.'

'We're only trying to give you some pleasure—and comfort,' said Sarah, her voice slightly ragged with restraint.

'Comfort?' repeated Uncle Donald. 'In ma ain hoose Ah'm as snug as a bug in a rug!'

At that Peter entered the kitchen with a parcel in his hand. 'Come on, Uncle Donald,' said Maisie. 'Here's your fish supper. You'll surely eat it after Peter going for it specially for you.'

'Naw. Ah never eat fish suppers excep' oota the same shop.'

'Well, how about bread and raspberry jam?' asked Sarah.

'Nae rasp jam fur me. The seeds gets in ablow ma fause teeth. Have ye nae treacle?'

'I'll look and see,' said Sarah, getting to her feet.

The visitor rose. 'Ach, don't bother. Ah'm fur away hame.'

'But ye cannae dae that!' protested his nephew. 'Ye're supposed tae bide here fur twa days.'

'Twa days? It wid kill me!'

'But, Uncle Donald!' pleaded Sarah, 'we're doing all we can. Sit down again and have tea. Maisie'll get your bath ready.'

'Naw-naw. Ah'm no' wantin' tae be droondit. Ah want tae go back tae ma ain hame.'

'What!' exclaimed Sarah; 'leave a nice house and go back to what's nothing better than a slum! We thought this would be a wee change. And anyway, Mattha and Biddy don't want you.'

'Naw,' said Willie, adding in his usual clumsiness, 'they're paperin' yer room. That's why they——'

'Paperin' ma room!' yelped Uncle Donald. 'Let me oota here. They've nae business interferin'. They've no' tae touch it!' He fumbled for his boots. 'Ah don't like chynges.'

Since he was so keen to go, and they were determined to please him, his departure was willingly hastened. What Mattha and Biddy said is outwith the genteel boundaries of this narrative.

Chapter 7

WHEN THE CAT'S AWAY

THE winter wore through to the month of January—a month during which all the members of the family fell victims to the common cold, Maisie's manifestation of it being so acute that she had to recuperate in the country. As her holiday drew near its end she wrote pleading with her mother to spend the last few days with her. A week away from home in the early days of February did not appeal to Sarah, but husband and son, for reasons best known to themselves, joined forces in persuading her to go. Her departure was accompanied by the usual last-minute instructions and last-minute switherings as to the advisability of going at all ; as it was also accompanied by last-minute assistance from Willie and Peter, Sarah was convinced that they were suspiciously anxious to be rid of her, and announced that she had a good mind not to go. In alarm Willie offered to carry her case to the bus.

'You'll do nothing of the kind,' came the retort. 'I'm not going to America. Now mind—if the water freezes——'

'We're to keep big fires on,' prompted Peter obligingly.

'No! *Wee* fires ! Oh dear, I'm sure the pair of you will do something daft.'

'Ach, don't heed him, Serah,' said Willie, edging her out of the kitchen. 'He's jist pullin' yer leg. Come on—gi'es a wee cheeper.'

Sarah drew back from the caress, her mind still tormented by the traditional male helplessness. 'Just a minute. That meat in the press there—don't eat it all at once, mind. What else now ? I suppose it'll be too much to expect you to have the house clean for Maisie and me coming back ? '

79

'Jist you wait!' exclaimed Willie, adding an extra ounce of push in the direction of the door. 'The hoose'll be that clean ye'll no' recognise it.'

But that was the wrong thing to say, it seemed. 'None of your impiddence!' stormed the reluctant traveller. 'And me in such a hurry. Well, I'm away. See and don't leave the wireless at full blast when you go to work in the morning. And mind—you're not to touch any of the tinned things!'

'Ah didnae ken there *wis* ony!' observed Willie. 'Whit else have we tae don't?'

'Oh, don't make a fool of me!' Sarah was on the verge of tears. 'I'm sure what I say just goes in one ear and out the other.'

'Well, of course, when there's nothing in between to stop it——' began Peter.

'Wheesht, son!' Willie's voice had the huskiness of a conspirator. 'Ye'll keep 'er back.' He had by this time managed to persuade his wife as far as the outside door; he opened it saying, 'Well, so long, hen. Tell Maisie Ah wis askin' fur 'er.'

She was out of the house now, on the landing, her face twisted with uncertainty and hurry and fear. 'You'll mind about the boiler?' she pleaded.

'What boiler?' asked Peter.

'Ach you!' snapped his father in exasperation and a great dread that something would come in the way of his plans for a week of complete freedom from wifely tyranny. 'The boiler behind the kitchen fire!' He propelled his dithering spouse towards the banisters. 'If ye don't run, hen, ye'll loss the train.'

She went down the stairs eventually, muttering that she wished she wasn't going. At the staircase window she stopped long enough to shout up, 'You'll not forget about the fire?' Husband and son assured her from the doormat that they would remember all her instructions; they retreated into the flat, Willie closing the door.

'Jeengs,' he gasped; 'Ah wis feart fur a meenit there she wisnae goin' efter a'. Boys-a-boys, Ah've been waitin' fur this

80

tae happen fur thirty year !' He rubbed his hands, slapped Peter on the back and exclaimed, 'Come on, son. We'll bring in the big easy chairs f'ae the parlour.'

'Just a minute. Let's roll up all the rugs in the kitchen first. They're just dirt-traps anyway.'

Together they bundled the rugs into the lobby press, took down the ornaments from the mantelpiece, looped back the curtains from the window, Willie singing all the while a tuneless ditty about his wife having gone to the country as 'she thought it best that I should rest, so now she's gone away.' He broke off to exclaim, 'Cheers ! We'll get pittin' wur feet on the mantelpiece an' spittin' on the ceilin' !'

'Yes, and sitting up till three in the morning without Mother wailing, "It's high time you two were in bed."'

Willie was in the act of turning to the wall the photographed face of his mother-in-law when the doorbell rang. Turning it face outwards again, he said, 'Ah bet ye that's hur back tae tell us no' tae keep big fires on !' But when he opened the door it was to find Sarah ready to step in, saying :

'I just felt I couldn't go away and leave you two poor souls all alone with nobody to look after you !'

Determination seized the man. Reaching for his cap on the hall-stand, he shouted for Peter to come and accompany him to the station. Against her will Sarah went too.

The following Thursday evening Peter and his father were at their supper—an informal affair with neither adornment nor comfort ; indeed, things had become so picnic-like that even Willie felt a remonstrance was justified.

'Here, Peter, whit wid yer mother say if she seen ye pittin' the fryin' pan on the table ?'

'Well, where can I put it ? The sink's choked with dishes and the grate's jammed up with pots——'

'Ach, pit it in the bunker. An' when ye're there, sling some coal on the fire.'

'I thought we weren't to keep big fires on. It's been freezing all day.'

'Ay, but the tap's still runnin'. There's nae danger as long as the b'iler's fu'. Pit on twa-three lumps onywey.'

'It's hardly worth while. It's near ten o'clock.' Peter's tones had a weariness that made his father retort :

'Ye're surely no' thinkin' o' yer bed a'readies ! You that wis fur steyin' up tae three in the mornin' ! '

'Ugh ! there's no fun staying up if you're not annoying anybody. Here, what about us washing some dishes tonight ? '

'Ach, whit's the hurry ? We havenae stertit on the weddin' china yet. Ye know the wey weemin are aye guddlin' wi' dish-washin' gets ma goat. You an' me'll hae a gran' fin-ally on Saturday. As soon as we've feenished wur dinner—Ah mean wur sausages—we'll get doon tae't. You can scrub the floor an' Ah'll wash the dishes an' things.'

'Will you do the grate ? '

'Ach, it'll no' need much. A slabber ower wi' a washin' cloot'll clean up the mess.'

'Who's to make the beds ? ' inquired Peter.

'Ach, we'll baith make wur ain,' answered his father generously.

'The place'll have to be dusted.'

'Away wi' ye—it cannae be that dusty efter jist a week ! '

'I think Mother dusts it every day,' said Peter dubiously.

'Here, there's nae need fur you tae make yer mother oot tae be worse nur she is ! '

While they made plans and argued the fire went out, so there was nothing for it but to go to bed, and Saturday afternoon was upon them before the accumulation of clamant housework had been tackled. They had only a few hours in which to perform tasks normally occupying the returning housewife for a whole week ; dinner, as a consequence, was gulped down half cooked, which meant, of course, half fried. Peter made several journeys to the ash-bins in the back court ; returning from one of them he found his father contemplating the kitchen bed from the grandstand viewpoint of the bed itself. Resisting the temptation to ask if he intended to lie down and die with his boots on, Peter got on with his allotted task of washing the kitchen floor, turning a deaf ear to the groanings emanating from the cupboard-like bed.

When the floor had been smeared with increasingly dirty water, Peter emptied the basin and offered to have a shot at making the bed.

'Right ye are,' said his father with alacrity. 'Every time Ah get one corner flat a bumphle comes at anither bit.' He left the seat of his exertions with a leap of joy, saying that he would get started to the washing of the dishes. En route for the scullery he remarked that he didn't think Peter had made a very good job of washing the kitchen floor. 'It's a' tidemarks!' he added.

'That's okay,' replied Peter calmly. 'The marks'll not show when you've polished it.'

'Polished? Me? Here—hiv you ony idea o' the dishes Ah've tae wash? Let alane pots?'

Peter did some swimming exercises on the sea of blankets. 'Ugh, keep your hair on!' he advised. 'I wish to goodness you'd let Mother keep the divan bed in here instead of shoving it in the sitting-room for the winter.'

Refusing to resurrect the buried hatchet which had been used some months before during a violent quarrel with his absent wife, Willie retorted, 'Ah cannae say ye're makin' ony less o' a habble o' that bed nur me.'

'Well, it's your fault!' Sudden resolve seized the bed-maker; one by one he tossed blankets on to the floor with more zeal than direction until Willie had to protest that the jam-pot was in danger. To which Peter replied that the table ought to have been cleared long ago.

'Ach, you!' Willie, conscience-stricken, removed himself and the jam-pot from the scene of operations, and went to put more coal on the fire with a view to having plenty of hot water for the washing of the mountain of dishes that had mysteriously turned up in all sorts of places. Peter wrestled with the bed with increasing futility, while his father tested the water in the scullery. It was hotter than he had ever known it before, and he was in the act of wondering how to make room for the washed dishes on the crowded draining-board when Peter called him:

'Dad—come here a minute. I've got an idea. You hold the

bed-clothes in front here, and I'll climb in to the back of the bed and flatten them.'

'Whit did Ah tell ye !' said Willie, leaving his sink problem unsolved and going to the bedside. 'You seemed tae think ye jist had tae whustle an' the blankets wid come-tae-ye-ma-lad.'

Peter, shoes and all, got to the back of the bed according to plan. According to plan he tucked the blankets in to his satisfaction, but there was an element of the unforeseen about his bringing some of the bed-clothes out again as he jumped out. When he had been disentangled from the mess and had assured his father he was not in any way damaged, they both concentrated on the task of disentangling five forks, two fish-supper papers, the remnants of their butter ration and the wrapping thereof, together with the other furnishings of the table that had not been cleared for a week. As a token of gratitude for the fact that his son was still sound in wind and limb, Willie offered to complete the making of the bed if Peter would wash the dishes.

'No fear !' said Peter, rubbing his elbow. 'I'm not putting my hands in water again today. They're all hacks with the frost. I tell you what—the steps !'

Willie gaped. 'Whi' d'ye want the steps fur ?'

Without answering, Peter disappeared into the lobby, returning with the article in question and, spreading it in front of the bed, he climbed to the top. 'Hand me over the window pole !' he commanded. Mystified, Willie could only obey, but he was full of admiration for the principle of Peter's new plan which was to hook the corner of the bed-clothes over the pole and, with an open-air draughts-board action, poke them one by one into position. Father and son surveyed the result.

'Fine !' announced Willie. 'A man wi' yae blin' e'e an' the ither yin stuffed wi' rags wid never think yer mother hadnae made it 'ersel'. Noo, let's sling the feather quilt ower the tap. There she goes ! Noo, come on. The dishes.'

Together they made for the scullery. 'Where's the dish-towel ?' asked Peter.

'Hoo should Ah know ?'

'It's a thin thing with a red border, isn't it ?'

Willie snocked about among the pots and pans beneath the sink and brought up a soggy mass. ' Will this be it ? ' he asked.

' No, that's what I washed the floor with.'

' Well, there's nae ither cloot here wi' a red border.'

Peter was aghast. ' Don't tell me I've used the wrong cloth.'

' Ach, jist dry it in front o' the fire,' suggested Willie. ' It'll no' take a meenit. Whit the eye disnae see——'

' I tell you what ! ' exclaimed Peter. ' The pillow-slips from my bed ! They're dirty anyway.' He was gone for them while Willie was in the middle of warning him to be careful not to break any dishes. He was back in time to hear him say :

' Yow ! That water's scaudin' me ! Yer mother's aye greetin' aboot it never bein' hot anuff—she disnae keep big anuff fires on—that's a'.'

But Peter was getting concerned about the shortage of time. ' They'll be here in ten minutes,' he estimated.

Willie dipped the cups in and out of the scalding water. ' They'll no' hauf be flabbergasted when they see the hoose sae spick an' span.'

' Mphm. The floor's washed anyway,' said the floor-washer.

' Ay—an' Ah dusted the dresser ! ' boasted his colleague, who yelped with pain as he added still more hot water to the basin in the sink. ' Yow ! Ma fing-ers'll be a' blisters.'

' Why don't you add some cold water ? ' asked Peter with sweet reasonableness.

' Ah cannae ! The folks doon the stair must be haein' a bath. The cold tap's been dry fur the last five meenits.'

' Eh ? ' The disastrous implication struck Peter with a smack. ' The water's frozen ! Holy smoke ! Look at the size of the fire ! '

They rushed to the grate, getting in each other's way as they danced before it in uncertainty how to cope with the situation. ' We'll have tae draw the fire ! ' yelled Willie.

Peter produced the shovel, demanding to know where they were to put the flaming coals.

' Ye'll hae tae run doon tae the midden wi' them.'

Handing over the shovel, Peter found another one in the

bunker ; Willie plied the tongs gingerly because of the fierce heat of the fire. The need for speed made him inept. At last, with one small cinder smoking on his shovel, he made for the door.

'Watch where you're going !' shouted Peter. 'Don't make a mess of my clean floor.'

Ignoring the warning, Willie announced they would have no time to go the length of the midden, two and a half flights below. 'We'll fling it on the stairheid,' he said, adding : 'Now you watch that dresser ! Ah dusted it.'

In a sort of torchlight procession they made for the door, dumped their smoking burdens on the stone stairs and were on their way back for more when a neighbour coming up the stair demanded to know what they were playing at. She insinuated that they were attempting to set fire to her doormat. The men had no time to argue with her and she was left shouting after them, 'I've a good mind to get the polis to you. Look at the mess ye're makin' of my nice clean stair. What are ye playin' at ?'

While she was yet speaking the procession reappeared. 'Should we pour cold water on it ?' asked Peter as he completed the pile.

'Naw, ye'd maybe get an explosion.'

The word 'explosion' was enough for the woman ; she raced down the stairs yelling, 'Help ! Fire ! Murder ! Polis !'

Shutting the door on the shouts, Peter stormed back to the kitchen saying, 'Surely there's something we can do—I don't want the boiler to burst and mess up my clean floor !'

But his concern was of no avail. With a preparatory hiss of steam the boiler yielded to the inevitable. His Home Guard training standing him in good stead, Willie pushed Peter before him in a rush for the protection of the bed as the soot-and-cinder storm rose and subsided. Suddenly the doorbell rang.

'Help ma boab !' exclaimed Willie, wiping his blackened face. 'That's yer mother an' Maisie at the door. Come on an' we'll lie doon on the floor an' let them come in wi' their key. They'll think we're hurtit an' we'll no' get a row.'

They lay on the floor that Peter had washed so carefully, the tidemarks now hidden beneath a dusting of lots of things; keeping silence, they awaited the maternal storm which they dreaded more than the one that had just passed. When the doorbell rang for a second time, it occurred to them that something was amiss. There was a fumbling at the letter-box on the outer door.

'I'll see what it is,' whispered Peter, and he crawled timorously to the door. He was back in a moment on his two feet.

'It's a telegram!' he exclaimed as he tore open the yellow envelope. 'It's from Mother!' He read it silently, then burst out: 'You can get up, Dad. Listen—she says, *Maisie sprained ankle. Stop. Staying till Monday. Stop. Don't keep big fires on.*'

Willie got to his feet. 'Guid auld Maisie!' he said fervently. In relief the two of them shook hands. Sufficient unto the day was the evil thereof.

CHAPTER 8

BETWEEN TWO FIRES

FOR fully a fortnight after his wife's return Willie conducted himself with due humility, but when the new boiler had been fitted to the kitchen range and the resultant mess cleaned up, his spirits soon recovered, and there came an evening when he felt sufficiently restored to normalcy to complain that he objected to being hustled away from the tea-table before he was finished with his newspaper.

'Oh, Willie, you *are* exasperating !' said Sarah. 'You know quite well Mrs M'Cotton's coming up tonight and I want the table cleared before she comes.'

'In that case,' exclaimed Peter, getting to his feet, 'I'm going out !'

'Ah think Ah'll go wi' ye,' commented Willie, without however making any movement from the table. 'That wumman gi'es me the bo——'

'Willie !' interjected Sarah. 'Don't be vulgar !'

'Well, she gi'es me the scunner, then, if ye think that's mair refined.' Clearing his throat, he emitted some unlovely noises meant to be in imitation of Mrs M'Cotton's speech : 'Good evening, Mr McFlehnnel. Isn't this naice weathah for this tehm of the yah.'

'Keep it up, Dad,' Maisie advised him. 'That sounds deadly, but in my opinion it's an improvement on your own version.' At which she in turn emitted some equally unlovely sounds meant to be in imitation of her father's speech : 'Hoo'ye, Mrs M'Coatt'n. Whit wey hiv ye no' brung yer man the night ?'

'That's enough, Maisie,' said Sarah. 'Come on, you, and

help me with the dishes. You know what Mrs M'Cotton is—always here half an hour before the time so's to catch you hiding something.'

Moving towards the scullery with her mother, the girl asked if the reason for the impending visit were known.

'It's supposed to be a jumper pattern she wants,' said Sarah, 'but it'll likely be to show off something new she's got. I don't know what I've ever done to deserve that woman for my daughter's mother-in-law.'

The girl felt the complaint a bit far-fetched but said nothing ; she was less vulnerable to attacks of the M'Cotton kind than her mother was, and in any case she could not bring herself to treating Mrs M'Cotton seriously.

'Maybe you'd better go and see what the sitting-room fire is like,' said Sarah before the dishes were all disposed of. 'I set a match to it about an hour ago.'

As Maisie left the kitchen, Peter wheedled, 'Mother—do Dad and I *need* to meet the M'Cotton ? '

Before Sarah could retort, the doorbell rang. 'Oh, would you believe it,' she moaned. 'That must be her already, and the tea dishes not all washed.'

'Dad and I can finish them,' suggested Peter eagerly.

Taking off her apron Sarah said she couldn't trust either of her men-folk with china ; then, as certain sounds filtered from the outside door to the kitchen, she paused while rolling up her apron. 'Oh,' she gasped, 'it's not Mrs M'Cotton after all ! It's your brother Mattha, Willie ! Of all the calamities ! '

Willie and Peter, glad to welcome anyone other than the expected visitor, were more than usually hearty in their greeting when Maisie flung open the door and announced, 'Cheer up, folks. It's not the M'Cotton Queen after all.'

'Hullo, Uncle Matt,' said Peter. 'You're just in time to help Dad and me with the dishes.'

'Oh, Ah'm nae use at that kinna thing,' said Mattha, dispensing with the formality of hand-shaking and seating himself unbidden in the most comfortable chair ; 'the wife jist synes oot oor dishes at the jawbox an' leaves them tae dreep tae the next meal. Oh, Ah'm glad tae get a sate. Ah've been on ma feet a' day.'

'Don't worry, Uncle Matt,' said Maisie sweetly. 'Mother and I are dab hands at " synin' things oot at the jawbox " too ! '

'Maisie—what a thing to say—and you a teacher !' ex-claimed the matter-of-fact Sarah.

'Ah doot she's tryin' fur tae get one in at me there,' put in the visitor, ' but Ah'm no' smert anuff tae see through it.'

'Come on, Maisie,' urged Sarah resuming her apron, ' and we'll get the job done before that woman comes.'

'Oh ? ' There was an element of disappointment in Mattha's voice. ' Wur yez expecin' visitors the night ? '

'Ay—thon wife M'Cotton,' said Willie. ' Serah an' hur's great pals. Eh, Serah ? '

'Oh, be quiet ! I can't bear you even to make a joke about it.'

'Judging by the parcel,' interposed Peter, ' I think Uncle Matt's up to sell us something.'

'Well, he needn't bother opening it,' said Sarah from the scullery, ' for we're not buying anything.'

'Ach, Serah, that's no' fair—efter me goin' tae the bother o' comin'.' Mattha stroked his parcel tenderly as he spoke. ' Feel it, Wullie—it's a terrible wecht.'

Willie obliged by feeling, and pronounced it to be so heavy that he would not care to have it drop on his corns. Mattha took the reference to corns to himself.

'Oh, don't *suggest* sichna thing,' he moaned.

'Well, what's in the parcel, Uncle Matt ? ' queried Peter. ' Are you travelling for dolls' eyes or railway tunnels ? '

'Now, Peter, you're not to encourage him,' exclaimed Sarah.

But Mattha, intent on conducting business, was already unwrapping his parcel. ' Wait tae ye see it, Serah,' he declared. ' It's the dandiest electric fire ye ever seen in yer life.'

'But we're not needing an electric fire ! '

Ignoring his sister-in-law's protestation, Mattha whipped away the crumpled paper covering the article, with as much aplomb as the most accomplished unveiler of statues, and stood back, saying, 'There—is that no' a real posh affair? Look, Serah. . . . Aw heh—it widnae cost ye onythin' jist tae *look* at it!'

Withholding her gaze Sarah insisted that she was having nothing to do with it.

Willie contemplated the electric fire from all angles. 'Ay?' he said. 'Whit's up wi't, Mattha?'

'There's naethin' up wi't! You're aye tryin' fur tae make oot Ah'm no' on the level. It's yin Ah got the chance o'.'

With apparent innocence, Peter inquired why the purchase had been made considering Uncle Matt did not have electricity in his flatlet.

'Ach, Ah jist minded on youse folks, an' Ah thocht it wis a peety fur youse tae hae sichna braw hoose an' still hae an auld-fashioned fireplace in yer pawrlur.'

The implication that there was something lacking in her housing scheme was too much for Sarah. 'Mattha McFlannel,' she exclaimed, 'don't you dare to sit there and criticise this house. It's a palace by's yours, and——'

'Aw Serah, hauf a chance!' pleaded Mattha. 'Ah didnae mean tae suggest yer hoose wisnae perfec'—it wis jist that, well . . . ehm . . .' His crafty mind groped after plausibility of expression: 'It's an awful posh electric fire, is't it no'?'

Willie spared his wife the necessity of giving a frank opinion by asking how much the thing had cost.

'Och well,' Mattha hedged, 'in the wey o' business, of coorse, Ah wid need tae get a wee profit fur ma bother——'

Pinning him down, Willie nipped in with: 'Ay, but hoo much wid it cost *us*?'

'Willie!' called Sarah in despair, 'we're not needing the thing!'

Peter, who had been fumbling with the coil of cord attached to the fire, remarked that he had not seen that type of cable for some time. Ignoring the lad, Mattha concentrated on Sarah.

'Ay but here, Serah, think hoo handy it wid be jist tae switch on an electric fire, supposin' somebody came up some night an' ye hadnae yer room fireplace redd oot.'

'My fireplaces are cleaned out first thing in the morning!'

'But it's a real bobby-dazzler, Serah. Look at the wee grid at the top here fur pittin' a kettle on—jist like a wee hob.' He stroked the grid lovingly ; 'It's a right smert wee contraption, so it is !'

'It looks pretty old-fashioned to me !' declared Sarah. 'All the newest ones are like scoops that reflect the heat.'

Mattha clucked with exasperation then turned to Maisie who had been sitting silently sewing by the fire : 'Heh, Maisie, are you no' interested in this braw electric fire ?' Getting a direct answer, he turned to Peter : 'Whit aboot you, then ? Ah heard ye were runnin' aboot wi' yer cousin f'ae Drumforber ? Ye micht be thinkin' o' settin' up hoose yin o' thae days——'

Before Peter's self-conscious blush had had time to show itself, Willie peered more closely at the article and asked if there were not a small chip evident in the enamel.

Mattha flicked the obvious blemish aside with : 'Ach that ? Ye could keep it in a corner an' that wee mark wid never be seen.'

'A radiator isn't much use in a corner,' said Sarah.

'Ye could stick a vauze o' flooers at the side, then,' was Mattha's retort.

From the fireside Maisie observed : 'The flowers wouldn't last long, would they ? Or does the fire not give off much heat ?'

'Naw ! Ah mean tae say—well, it widnae be that hot at the side.'

'I think,' said Sarah, 'you should parcel it up again, Mattha. Take it home and keep it till you get electricity in your own house.'

'Oh but Ah widnae go in fur that style o' radiator— Ah mean, we'll maybe no' get electricity in fur years yet.'

Perceiving the extent of his brother's perversity, Willie accused him of being a twister and ordered him angrily to take the fire off the premises immediately, a suggestion that grieved Mattha.

'Aw heh, Wullie,' he moaned, 'that's a fine-like thing fur tae say tae yer ain flesh an' blood. Ah widnae of came if Ah hadda knew yez wid of been sae meanjie.'

Peter drowned his mother's protest by demanding to know how much Mattha had paid for it.

' Whit's that got tae dae wi't ? ' snapped the scrap merchant.
' It's a dirty shame, so it is, bringin' me up here an' it sichna
weight an' me wi' sich sair corns.'

' Nobody asked you to come,' Sarah pointed out.

Trying kindness, Willie said : ' Ach, row it up again, Mattha,
an' away hame wi' ye. The shop'll take it back if ye say yer
customer didnae want it efter a'.'

' Ah didnae get it in a shop, but ! Ah mean. . . .' He tried
again : ' Ach Serah, Ah tell ye whit—Ah'll gie ye it cost price—
without a penny profit tae me fur a' ma bother. Whit d'ye say—
three-pound-ten tae you, Serah.'

' But I'm telling you I don't need an electric fire ! I don't
think they're healthy. I always feel they dry up the atmosphere
in a room.'

' Well, ye could aye keep a bowl o' watter doon in front o't.'

' Susan wid drink it,' said Willie.

Mattha brushed his brother aside : ' Here's anither thing, Serah.
Say you're haein' visitors—ye've got tae light yer room fire a
coupla hours afore they come, an' if ye're lum's no' swep'——'

' I get all my chimneys swept regularly ! '

' Aw, Mattha, gi'e it up,' advised Willie.

But Mattha pursued his sales talk : ' Well, then, say it's a
windy night, an' the fire'll no' light, an' the room's fu' smoke
cos yer sticks is wet——'

' I never try to light a fire with wet sticks.'

' Well, whit aboot back-smoke f'ae the wife next door ? '

Sarah faced him squarely : ' I don't see how an electric fire
in my room would help back-smoke from the one next door.'

' Try another tack, Uncle Matt,' suggested Peter. ' Tell her
she'd not have corns on her knees lighting fires if she bought a
radiator.'

' Aw, Peter,' Mattha mopped his brow mournfully, ' if you
suffered as much as me wi' corns on yer feet, ye widnae be makin'
jokes aboot haein' them on yer knees.'

At that moment the doorbell rang and Sarah bethought her of
her expected visitor. ' Oh, Mrs M'Cotton ! ' she gasped.

' Will I go ? ' asked Peter.

'No-no. You stay here and keep your Uncle Mattha's mind occupied !'

Willie called after her retreating figure : 'Heh, Serah, whit aboot bringin' 'er in here an' maybe Mattha could sell the electric fire tae hur ?'

'Don't be silly !' She drew the kitchen door after her firmly and went to the outside door feeling sorry for herself. It was bad enough to be saddled with a disreputable relative-in-law like Mattha, but it was worse that he should come into contact with her genteel enemy. She admitted the lady without any visible sign of warmth, Mrs M'Cotton, for her part, being frigidly polite. She expressed the opinion that Sarah was looking rather washed-out.

Sarah insisted that she was perfectly well and guided her visitor towards the sitting-room.

'Are we not going into the kitchen as usual ?' asked Mrs M'Cotton.

'No,' said Sarah trying to sound casual. 'There's a good fire in here.' But her words were proven false for when she opened the door there was a dead blackness in the grate. 'Maisie !' she shouted. 'Come here ! The fire's gone out !'

Maisie came speeding from the kitchen conference, greeted the latest visitor cursorily and then reminded her mother that she had been on her way to inspect the sitting-room fire when she had had to stop and admit Uncle Mattha. 'We'll all just have to sit in the kitchen,' she concluded.

'What ! And Uncle Mattha there !'

Mrs M'Cotton could not but surmise the meaning of the glance with which Sarah accompanied her ejaculation. She said :

'If Eh wasn't so tied up with engagements, Eh'd suggest coming some other evening, but as it is——'

'Maisie,' said Sarah, cross with vexation, 'get some papers and sticks and we'll set this fire going again.'

'Oh, Eh'll be all right in meh fir coat,' said the visitor preening herself, 'but of course you might feel the cold in that thin frock, Mrs McFlehnnel. That's the wirst of these utility things—there's no heat in them.'

Sarah made no attempt to hide her feelings when she retorted :
' It's *not* utility. Maisie—get the sticks, please ! '

In the doorway Maisie hesitated : ' Um . . . I was just
wondering—what about testing out the electric fire that's been
on show——'

' Don't say electric fire to me ! ' snapped Sarah.

The girl departed. Mrs M'Cotton put her head on one side
and contemplated her hostess.

' Dear me, Mrs McFlehnnel,' she said, ' you're very narrow-
minded, surely. Eh always think an electric fehr is *such* a con-
venience. Meh friend Mrs McVelvet's got a new one—oh, a
marvellous thing it is—it's a fehr-screen when it's not in use.
Most artistic ! But of course, all her furniture's modern. It
would look odd in an old-fashioned room like this ! '

Sarah's gulp of amazement went unnoticed in the commotion
caused by Willie rushing into the room demanding : ' Heh,
Serah, whit's this aboot the fire bein' oot ? Hoo'ye, Mrs
M'Cotton. Could Mattha no' bring——'

' Don't you dare to suggest Mattha coming in here ! ' Sarah's
observation was almost a shout. ' Mrs M'Cotton's here ! '

Just then Maisie followed her father into the room, carrying
a handful of paper and firewood.

' Eh do wish you wouldn't fuss,' said Mrs M'Cotton. ' Eh'm
quate warm and it'll take hours to heat up the room.'

At that Mattha joined the procession, having heard the remark.
' That's whit Ah wis sayin', Serah,' he began.

Sarah turned on her husband. ' Willie ! ' she almost screamed ;
' will you take that brother of yours out of here ! '

Mattha, however, showed no more inclination to be led away
than Willie showed to be his escort. ' Aw, Serah, Ah wis jist
tryin' fur tae help ye ! ' he protested. Turning to Mrs M'Cotton
he addressed that lady in terms so familiar that she might have
been wearing a cloth coat instead of the synthetic fur variety she
favoured. ' Hoo'ye, Mrs M'Cotton,' he said ingratiatingly.
' Ah've seen ye manys a time on the street, but Ah don't think
ye've noticed me. Ah'm Wullie's brither.'

' Eh'm quate well aware of thet fect,' said the lady coldly.

95

Sarah, torn between shame of Mattha, dislike of Mrs M'Cotton, chagrin at the fire's behaviour, fear of the potentialities as represented by Mattha, laid a persuasive hand on a synthetic fur sleeve. 'I tell you what, Mrs M'Cotton,' she said. 'You and I can go into the kitchen and the rest can stay here. Come on.'

'Aw, haud yer horses, Serah,' protested Willie. 'Ye're no' gonnae leave us tae sit in a cauld room !'

'It widnae be cauld,' Mattha hastened to point out, 'if ye wis tae let me plug in that electric fire.'

Sarah ignored him : 'Are you coming, Mrs M'Cotton ?'

But the lady lingered : 'Eh think Eh'd rather stay here, Mrs McFlehnnel. Eh'm not used with sitting in a kitchen, you know.'

Once again Mattha was on his conversational toes. 'That's whit Ah've been sayin', Serah. A braw room like this should be sat in—no' pit-by fur a guid thing !'

From the door Sarah thanked Mattha in advance for the small service of keeping his opinions to himself, but although Mattha immediately fell on his knees it was more in a spirit of inquiry than of gratitude. When questioned on the subject he admitted he was looking for an electric point in the skirting board. Peter who had also joined the parlour party was quick to say that there was a plug behind the piano—a statement hailed by his uncle with delight and his mother with fury. While she was still berating the lad for sabotage of the home-front, Mattha called on Willie to help him shift the piano ; this in turn resulted in a frank exchange of opinion between husband (who was not above a little light entertainment) and wife (who was not above expressing herself with complete frankness).

'Oh, Eh'm so glad,' exclaimed Mrs M'Cotton with apparent truthfulness, 'Eh came here toneght. Eh do enjoy listening to a femly quarrel. Mr McFlehnnel's brother is so quaint !'

Mattha interpreted this as a compliment. 'That's real kind o' ye, missus !' he said.

The information that the name was M'Cotton was rather lost in Sarah's shouted insistence that Peter was not to lend a hand in the shifting of the piano's position, as was also Mattha's remark that the electric point was in a gey queer position. But in spite

96

of everything, Mattha won. He crawled in between the dislodged instrument and the wall, located the point at issue and yelled for someone to bring him the radiator plug. This did not take long since it appeared Mattha had taken the precaution of bringing the combination into the room with him.

Said Peter : ' I didn't know they sold new radiators with plugs attached to them.'

' Ach but this is an extra special kind,' retorted Mattha from behind the piano.

Meanwhile the radiator sat in the middle of the room, naked and unashamed. Mrs M'Cotton exclaimed :

' Dear me, Mrs McFlehnnel, you're surely not thinking of behing an old-fashioned thing like that ! If Eh'd known you were as poor as all thet, Eh could of let you hev one Eh was going to throw out. It's a much more modern design than thet—it's the copper-bowl tehp ! '

Sarah's protests punctuated this speech, but Mattha's voice, being stronger, penetrated first : ' Ay, but ye couldnae bile a kettle on yer bowl-type—it wid be ower shoogly. Is it thon kind wi' the element stickin' straight up f'ae the middle o' the bowl ? '

' Yes, of course ! '

' Ach, there's nae heat affa that kind ! '

' It would give off plenty of heat for this small room ! ' insisted Mrs M'Cotton. ' Eh must bring it down to you, Mrs McFlehnnel. Or if Peter would come along——'

' Once and for all, Mrs M'Cotton, I don't want an electric fire—either Mattha's kind or yours ! ' Sarah's looks added exclamation marks to her words.

' Dear me, Mrs McFlehnnel, Eh wouldn't of thought you would of been so out of date in your ideas. There's nothing to beat an electric fehr. It's so economical and so clean——'

Mattha, sensing that a rival ' in the wey o' business ' had arrived on the scene, turned his back on his task of persuading the plug to fit into the point and applied himself to the more urgent problem.

' That's jist whit Ah wis sayin' tae ye, Serah. Economical an' clean.'

Before Sarah could retort, Mrs M'Cotton got in with : ' Mrs McFlehnnel, you *must* let me give you thet old one of mehn. It won't cost you anything, you know. Eh know how difficult it must be for you to make ends meet these days——'

Sarah was too insulted to stem the torrent of Mattha's counter-speech. ' But this yin's faur better, Serah. Look, if ye don't want the hale thing het up, ye jist need tae switch on one o' the elements. An' there's this wee hob forbye.'

' You'd just be throwing your money away, Mrs McFlehnnel,' said Mrs M'Cotton, ' if you took thet miserable-looking thing. You'd be far better with mehn. Eh was just going to throw it out anyway.'

' Thank you, but I don't need to be indebted to anybody for their cast-offs ! ' said Sarah.

This statement Mattha took to be a capitulation in his direction. With great delight, he said, ' Then ye'll take this yin, Serah. Ah kenned ye wid. It's a bargain ! '

' It's a swindle ! ' said Mrs M'Cotton.

' Here—don't you talk tae me like that ! ' roared Mattha, his voice no doubt magnified with the aid of the sounding-board against which he was jammed. ' Ah'm as honest as yer ain man —an' as fur yer faither——'

Astonished at his knowledge of her antecedents, Mrs M'Cotton could only blurt out, ' What do you know about my father ? ' but there was more fear than curiosity in the tone.

' Plenty ! ' declared Mattha.

Between the man's anxiety to impart some information and her own anxiety to avoid disclosures, Mrs M'Cotton was forced to her feet. ' I'm not staying here to be insulted ! ' she announced. For once, Sarah was reluctant to see her go.

' Oh, you'll need to wait and have a cup of tea,' she said, but although Willie added his assurances that they could all be doing with a cup of tea, the owner of the fur coat refused to be delayed. What her departure lacked in dignity it more than made up for in haste. It was not, the family recalled, the first occasion on which she had made a similar exit.

The outer door closed, Mattha applied himself to his worshipful attitude once more, but the deity at whose shrine he appeared to be in adoration must have been displeased with him for there was a sudden flash which was followed by engulfing darkness. Her mouth open to ask Mattha for details regarding Mrs M'Cotton's family history, Sarah was the first to give expression to the obvious by saying that the lights were out.

'It's a fuse!' announced Peter with equal lack of originality.

For a while Mattha tried to argue that the fault lay with the quality of the current supplied to the flat, alternatively with the inefficiency of the tradesman who had installed the point; but his protests were in vain. Sarah, groping towards the light of the kitchen fire, shouted:

'If you don't take that radiator out of this house this very minute, I'll get Peter to go for the police.'

'Aw, Serah,' pleaded Mattha. 'Ah'll gie ye it fur a pound.' This being greeted with silence, he added: 'Ten shillin's, then?' Finally, no response coming from the kitchen, he roared: 'Ah'll gie ye it fur whit it cost me! Five bob!'

His confession was his complete undoing. In the darkness Willie groped for the *corpus delicti*; seizing it and his brother he stumbled towards the outer door. The stairhead light seemed to burn with extraordinary brightness, but it was the outer darkness as far as Mattha was concerned.

Two days later Sarah purchased an up-to-date model of electric fire; true, it lacked some of the salient features of the one owned by Mrs M'Cotton's friend Mrs McVelvet, but with it Sarah felt she could face any onslaught that might come to her from either of her enemies.

CHAPTER 9

SUSPECTS

RETURNING from shopping one afternoon, Sarah met her next-door neighbour, Mrs M'Corduroy, on the common stairway. For a few minutes they stood talking, their conversation ranging over the well-trodden fields of the weather and their respective husbands' shortcomings. They were on the point of parting when Mrs M'Corduroy remembered something.

' Oh, I nearly forgot to tell you—you had a visitor this afternoon.'

' A visitor ? ' queried Sarah, her thoughts stumbling wildly over possibilities.

' Yes—a policeman. I'd been out with the dog and when I came up the stair I met him coming down. He asked me if I was Mrs McFlannel, and I said no. He said you must be out but he'd be back in the evening.'

Sarah was appropriately aghast. ' Good gracious ! What on earth would a policeman want with me ? '

' You'll need to be careful, Mrs McFlannel,' teased the other woman. ' Are you sure you haven't been making whisky on the sly ? '

Ignoring the suggestion, Sarah demanded to know if the policeman had revealed the cause of his visit.

' He didn't give away a cheep. He was going down the stairs when he turned back to ask how many of a family you had.'

' You didn't tell him, did you ? '

' Of course I did. I didn't think there was anything to hide. I said your husband was a foreman in the shipyards and Maisie was a teacher and Peter a radio engineer.'

' Did you say anything about Matt ? '

' Well, I admitted he was in the Navy.'

' I wonder what it can be,' said Sarah, clutching at the neck of her jumper. ' Did he take a note of what you said ? '

' I didn't notice him writing anything down, if that's what you mean. He just said he'd call back in the evening and did I think you'd be at home.'

' Oh dear-dear,' wailed Sarah with a certain lack of originality, ' what dreadful thing has happened ? '

' Cheer up, Mrs McFlannel,' advised Mrs M'Corduroy. ' If you've got to go to prison, I'll bake you a cake with a file in it.'

But Sarah could not be expected to see the point of her neighbour's hilarity. ' Prison ! ' she gasped. ' Oh this is terrible ! Are you sure he didn't give you any idea . . . ? '

' Not the slightest ! Come on, buck up ! ' Seeing the genuine distress she had caused, Mrs M'Corduroy patted Sarah on the shoulder : ' If you've got to face trouble it won't do to lose your nerve.'

' Oh, I'll need to get into the house ! ' gulped Sarah. ' I hope Maisie's home. This is awful. Oh dear-dear ! '

Without having the heart to make formal farewells, Sarah fumbled for her key and almost fell into the house, shouting :

' Maisie ! Maisie ! Are you in ? '

The girl came running from the scullery announcing that she had just put the kettle on.

' Never mind the kettle ! Oh, Maisie—something dreadful's happened ! The police were here this afternoon looking for me.'

' Looking for *you* ? ' The unbelief could not be mistaken.

' Yes—I met Mrs M'Corduroy on the stair and she told me he'd been here and he's coming back tonight.'

' Good heavens, Mother !—have you been witnessing an accident ? '

' Not that I remember. Oh, let me sit down. My legs are shaking ! '

Sarah sat down while Maisie hovered over her. ' Now don't get all jittery, Mother. Keep calm and try to think if you saw somebody that looked like a burglar running in the street or anything like that.'

'No-no, Maisie. I'm sure I never. I—I . . . d'you know the first thing that came into my head when she said there had been a policeman at the door—yon eggs we got from Drumforber last month. Maybe they've found out. Oh, Maisie, I wish I'd never taken them.'

'Look here, Mother, you've nothing to worry about in that direction. Aunt Bella has only seven hens and she doesn't need to send her eggs to the Pool.'

'I know, but I'm quite sure it's against the law to take them all the same. Oh, get me a drink of water. I'm feeling awful queer.'

Maisie fetched the water with the remark that the police were far too busy to be chasing up all the half-dozens of eggs that might pass between one sister and another.

'Oh, but somebody's always being caught ! And it won't be just me that'll get into trouble—it'll be Bella as well—and think what a disgrace that would be in a wee place like Drumforber. Oh dear-dear, I should never have taken them, but it's such a treat to get fresh eggs. Oh Maisie . . .' Sarah broke down completely so that it was with difficulty her words could be understood : 'Fancy if I've to go to prison ! '

'Mother, you're just letting your imagination run away with you ! Even if it *was* that, I'm quite sure you wouldn't need to go to prison ! ' Contemptuously she added : 'Half a dozen eggs ! '

'But how could they have found out ?' Sarah moaned.

Without replying, Maisie took the empty tumbler and offered to help her mother to take off her hat and coat. Allowing herself to be disrobed, Sarah continued, 'Oh, what a disgrace it'll be for you with the other teachers, Maisie, if your mother's to go to prison ! '

Maisie laughed softly and kissed her mother, not quite sure how to treat the situation.

Weeping, Sarah acknowledged the kiss with the statement that her daughter was far too kind to her. 'Oh, I don't know what your father'll say to this. He'll never forgive me ! He didn't want me to take the eggs and he won't forget to tell me that ! Oh, Maisie—Maisie——'

'There-there, Mother, pull yourself together and try to tell me all that Mrs M'Corduroy told you. Maybe you've picked her up wrongly.'

Sarah repeated, with frequent pauses to wipe her eyes, the story Mrs M'Corduroy had told her. When she came to the part about the policeman getting information as to the occupations of the various members of the family, Maisie felt it was time to call a halt and to ask if Mrs M'Corduroy, out of her natural gift for imparting news, had supplied answers to direct questions or had given the particulars gratuitously. Sarah, reflecting, said that she was sure the policeman had had to drag the information out of a reluctant Mrs M'Corduroy. Her memory, however (or was it her excitement?), was at fault when she added, 'She said he wrote it all down in his notebook, and he said he was coming back tonight to make an arrest.'

'Arrest?' Maisie was thoroughly shaken at last. 'Are you sure?'

'Positive.'

'I wonder . . .' It was Maisie's turn now to grasp the neckline of her jumper. 'Good heavens!'

Something in the girl's manner caused Sarah to gasp, 'What?'

'It's just occurred to me—one of the teachers in the school offered to get me a book of clothing coupons for three pounds. I'm so desperately short I—I—was considering it. Good grief!'

'Oh, Maisie! I'd rather it was the eggs than it should be anything to do with you,' said Sarah self-sacrificingly. 'If you had to go to prison you'd lose your job.'

'But there can't be any question of going to prison for that sort of thing! Or can there? My gosh—it puts the wind up me! Why the heck did I ever even discuss the idea. I knew quite well.'

'But you didn't actually *buy* the book, did you?'

'No, but I promised to take the money to school tomorrow. Oh, Mother!' Maisie looked round for a chair to collapse into. 'Isn't it awful. The police must've got wind of it.'

'But where was the clothing book to come from?'

'Oh, don't ask me. It was to be a terrible secret. The irony of it is that coming home tonight I made up my mind I wasn't going to have anything to do with the affair! Gosh—what a mess!'

Just then there was a banged door and a whistle which announced the homecoming of Peter. Sarah got to her feet, exclaiming that the tea was not even set; she further observed that she, personally, did not feel like eating, a sentiment that Maisie echoed.

'Hallo, what's up?' demanded Peter, aware of the electricity of the atmosphere as well as the pale faces of his women-folk.

'We've had bad news,' said Maisie.

'Yes,' agreed Sarah. 'You better tell him the whole thing, Maisie.'

But Maisie declined the task, offering instead to get on with preparing the neglected meal.

'There was,' said Sarah, with a sigh and an unconscious groping after dramatic effect, 'a policeman at the door this afternoon when I was out. But he got the hold of Mrs M'Corduroy and she told him to come back tonight when we'd all be in.'

'What did he want?' asked Peter, obligingly giving his mother an opportunity to draw her breath.

'I thought at first it must be me he was after, because of the eggs I got from Drumforber, but now Maisie thinks it's her—she got the offer of a book of clothing coupons for three pounds.'

Peter whistled.

'The policeman seems to have wormed everything out of Mrs M'Corduroy—all about what you all worked at and whether we made whisky in the house or not.'

'Oh, but that's nonsense, Mother,' said Peter with a laugh. 'She must've been pulling your leg.'

'No, she wasn't! She said he wrote it all down in his note-book and he's coming back tonight to make an arrest. I'm glad Matt's not home on leave just now so he can't be mixed up in this. But what a disgrace this'll be to him when he hears about it.'

'Come on, Mother,' said Peter sympathetically enough.

'Don't let yourself go!' Then, as a sudden thought came to him, he drew in his breath sharply and stammered, 'Gug-good heavens! I've ju-just thought of something!'

'Oh, Peter—don't say *you*'ve done something wrong next!' said Maisie, pausing in the tea preparations.

'It was this morning—in the bus,' said the lad. 'I was reading a new book on photography and I didn't notice I'd gone past my stop. When I got down to the platform an inspector gave me a telling-off for going beyond my ticket. Said the Corporation was going to make an example of somebody. The blighter must've followed me to my work.'

'Good grief!' was all Maisie could say; her mother, however, was more loquacious.

'Cheating the Corporation! Oh, this is dreadful! What next! I wish your father was home!'

'Ugh,' said Maisie, finding her voice, 'this is getting beyond a joke. The whole affair is assuming the proportions of a farce. I'm getting on with making the tea. And I think, Mother, you'd feel a lot better if you did something too. Keep your mind occupied.'

That, however, Sarah regarded as an insult. 'Maisie! How can you be so heartless? Here's me just crazy with worry, and you tell me to keep my mind occupied.' The tears were sprouting again.

'I don't feel too good myself!' retorted Maisie. 'Come on, Mother, Dad'll be here any minute, and he'll be crying out loud if his tea's not ready. What's for tea anyway?'

'Oh, I just can't think of food and this hanging over us!' wailed Sarah; turning to Peter, she added, 'Oh, d'you know, son, I'd far rather it was the eggs.'

Peter, wilfully misunderstanding her, said, 'Well, eggs are okay by me—provided they're boiled three at a time.'

'But, Peter, it's not eggs for tea I mean—it's the eggs I got from your Aunt Bella. Maybe the police have found out and I've to go to prison for them.'

Peter's retort was lost in the bustle that announced the arrival of the head of the house. The man came into the kitchen, took one look at his woebegone wife and asked who had stolen her scone.

' Oh, Willie, don't laugh at me—and the policeman coming up to arrest me ! '

' Whit the . . .' Willie gaped from one to the other of his worried family. ' Here—whit's up ? '

Sarah burst into tears which Maisie tried to stem by saying, ' There-there, Mother. It's far more likely to be me ! I've done a worse thing than you ! '

' What about me ? ' asked Peter.

' Heh, will some o' ye tell me whit's goin' on here ? ' suggested Willie.

Once again Sarah gave a ring-side description. ' There was a policeman here this afternoon looking for us. I was out, but he cross-examined or whatever you call it Mrs M'Corduroy, and he's coming back tonight to arrest somebody, and I'm sure it's me because of those eggs you wanted me to get from Drumforber.'

The unfounded allegation was too much for Willie. ' Me— wanted you tae take them ? Ah never done nae sich thing ! Ah tellt ye at the time ye were breakin' the law. Ah'm haein' naethin' adae wi' the affair. Whit wey's the tea no' ready ? '

' Oh, how can you think about food ? ' demanded Sarah, ' and this terrible thing hanging over our heads—me maybe going to prison. Oh, Willie ! '

Willie declined the offer of a damp face wherewith to adorn his shoulder. ' But hoo dae ye ken the polis wis lookin' fur *you* ? It micht be Peter here that he's efter, fur throwin' matches intae pillar-boxes or somethin'.'

' It's more likely to be me, Dad,' put in Maisie. ' I got the offer of a book of clothing coupons and I nearly bought them.'

' Help ma boab—Ah never knew Ah wis bidin' wi' a gang o' crooks ! This is a fine-like cairry-on ! Hoo am Ah gonnae haud up ma heid in the work if you an' yer mother's got tae go tae jile ? '

' Oh, Willie,' sniffed Sarah, ' do you not lul-love me any more ? '

'Aw, Serah, don't talk aboot love at a time like this ! Can ye no' run away an' hide somewhere ? Whit aboot goin' up tae Drumforber till it blaws by ? '

'But they might look for me there—that's where I got the eggs ! '

'Here, Dad,' said Peter, ' are you sure there's no chance the bobby was looking for you ? '

'Whit ? ' Indignation straightened the man's shoulders.

'Peter ! Don't talk like that to your father ! ' commanded Sarah.

'Well, he's got as much chance of something guilty up his sleeve as the rest of us ! '

'Well, ye're wrang there ! ' replied Willie in self-righteous complacency. ' Catch *me* buyin' eggs an' clothin' coupons in the Black Market ! '

Protests came from two quarters : Sarah's was a simple denial that the eggs were anything other than a present, while Maisie's was more complicated owing to the fact that she cited as a proof of her innocence her intention to have nothing to do with the transaction.

'And,' added Peter, ' I don't make a habit of going past my bus stop.'

'Help ma boab ! ' ejaculated Willie at this further evidence of his family's perfidy. ' Are you in it forbye ? It's a peety Matt's no' here—maybe ye could blame somethin' on him an' a' ! '

Mention of Matt's name drew a gasp from Sarah. ' Oh ! Matt ! Maybe that's what it is ! Maybe something's happened to Matt and the policeman was up to tell us. I never thought of that ! '

'Ach, fur the luva mike stop gettin' a' het-up aboot things. Ye're jist lettin' yer imagination run away wi' ye ! ' declared Willie impatiently. ' Come on an' get ma tea on the table Ah'm that hungry Ah could eat a scabby——'

'Willie—don't be vulgar ! ' shrieked Sarah ; ' and me so worried about Matt ! Maybe he's lying dud-dead at the bub-bottom of the sea. Oh, my poor wee Matt ! '

Willie gazed at his grief-stricken imagination-ridden wife.

'Here, Serah,' he roared, ' if ye don't get a move on wi' ma tea Ah'll need tae muck-in at the piece ye gi'en me this mornin'.'

Unimpressed by what was meant to be a knock-out blow, Sarah could only moan, ' Oh dear-dear,' but her grief was all for her sailor son. Willie, however, took the lamentation to his own behalf.

'Ach, ye don't need tae be sorry fur me. Ah had a guid dinner at the canteen.'

' I wasn't being sorry for you—I was thinking about Matt ! '

'Ah took a sudden staw at sangwidges,' continued Willie, still on his own behalf.

'Well, Dad,' said Maisie, ' you'd better fetch them and put them on the table. They'll have to be eaten tonight or they'll be all dried up.'

'Ach, they'll be a'right,' said Willie indifferently. ' Ma attachy case wis never opened f'ae the time Ah left the hoose this mornin'.'

' All the same, we'll eat the sandwiches just now,' said Maisie firmly.

'Well, mind, Ah'll no' take ony o' the flask tea the noo.'

'Okay,' conceded the deputy housekeeper ; ' but we can't waste bread.'

Deciding to stop worrying on his own account, Peter offered to bring the unopened attaché case from the lobby where, presumably, it had been left by Willie in a spot most likely to be awkward for the unwary. Willie turned once more to his wife.

'Come on, Serah. Screw aff the watter-works. Ah never knew onybody that could get sichna lota misery oota 'er imagination. Maybe the polis wis jist up tae tell ye Matt had been made a captain.'

But this was no comfort. Sarah nursed her misery lest it die of neglect, scarcely lifting her head when Peter returned with the attaché case, remarking that his father didn't half carry a heavy ' piece.'

'Ay—Ah wis jist thinkin' it wis heavier nur usual the day,' Willie agreed. ' Maybe it wis that that pit the notion in ma heid fur haein' ma dinner in the canteen.'

Peter put the case on the table, while Maisie hurried off to the scullery to fetch crockery and cutlery. The case open, Peter gaped at its contents.

'Dad—what's this you've got here?'

'Whit? Where?'

'This isn't your piece!'

Willie in turn gaped at the yawning receptacle. 'Jeengs! Whit's that?'

'That,' said Peter, 'is a tidy set of burglar's tools!'

In the background Sarah fought with a fainting fit which went unattended as far as the men were concerned. From the scullery Maisie yelled:

'Look out! Mother's fainting!'

'Tae hang wi' hur!' said the devoted husband; 'whit's thae burglar's tools daein' in ma case?'

Maisie rushed to her mother's side in time to hear her feeble whisper, 'That's what the policeman was after.'

Peter enumerated the items: 'Keys, a jemmy, a screw-driver——'

Stopping the inventory, Willie demanded, 'But hoo the bleezes did thae things get intae ma case?'

'But it's not your case, Dad,' said Peter. 'Look—yours hasn't got those safety locks on it.'

'Help ma boab!'

'You've been framed, Dad,' was Peter's transatlantic observation, delivered with some smugness.

'Oh, Willie,' came the moan from the background, 'what will the neighbours think if you've got to go to prison.'

'Prison, yer granny!' said Willie, without looking round. 'Ah'm takin' thae things tae the polis office afore Ah get ma tea!'

'Did you leave your case down anywhere, Dad?' asked Maisie, whose favourite literature was detective fiction.

Willie pondered. 'Naw. Ah had it on ma knee a' the wey hame in the bus the night. An' Ah had it in ma locker at the work. . . .' He scratched his head. 'Wait! It wis this mornin' in the bus! Ah had tae staun' a' the road, so Ah pit it ablow the stair.'

'Mphm!' said Peter. 'And somebody swopped cases with you. As I said—you've been framed!'

'Oh, Willie,' said Sarah in a fresh access of grief, 'this is terrible. How could you have been so stupid as not to notice the difference in the two cases.'

At that moment the doorbell rang and even Willie got a shock, for he exclaimed, 'Help—the polis! An' me wi' the burglar's tools on me!'

Sarah sprang to life. 'Throw the case out of the window!' she shouted. 'Willie—you'll need to hide—under Maisie's bed or in the lobby press or somewhere.'

'Hide?' repeated Willie. 'Whit d'ye take me fur? A wean at a pairty?'

'But, Willie, think of the disgrace!'

'I'm going to open the door,' said Maisie, 'but remember, Dad, whatever happens—I still like you a wee bit.' Kissing the dumbfounded man's cheekbone, she disappeared into the lobby.

'Whit the bleezes is she goin' slobberin' ower me like that fur—as if Ah wis gonnae get hung?'

The words were hardly out of his mouth before his wife had flung herself upon him. 'Oh, Willie, my poor Willie! Will they take you away in a Black Maria and it not dark yet?'

Peter pulled his mother from her unreciprocated embrace. 'Come on, buck up! Don't let the bobby see you're upset.'

Flopping down in her chair once again, Sarah made a brave effort to control herself as the door was flung open and Maisie announced:

'Well, folks, here we are. Here's Mr Policeman—and it's Dad he wants to see.'

Sarah hid her begrutten features in her handkerchief once again, while Willie squared his shoulders and said, 'Well, here Ah am. But mind ye, Ah never done it!'

The policeman laughed. 'Good evening, Mr McFlannel. Dad said you'd be sure to crack a joke about me coming to see you.'

'Your Dad?' came from three directions.

'Yes—you'll remember him in the Home Guard, Mr McFlannel. McSerge is the name.'

'McSerge?' Willie's reply was guarded. 'Ay—Ah mind 'im fine ! But whit does he ken aboot it ? '

'Nothing, really, but he thought that you might be willing to buy one or two tickets for the Police Concert next week.'

'Police Concert ? ' Sarah was the first to find her voice. 'Then you aren't going to arrest us ? '

'Of course not ! However did you get that idea ? '

'Well, Mrs M'Corduroy next door said you took a note of all our names.'

The young fellow laughed. 'I only asked about the family so's I could have an idea how many tickets you'd want.'

Willie mopped his head. 'Help ma boab—an' me a' worked up aboot goin' tae jile. But Ah wisnae as worried as the wife ! '

'Then you don't know anything about these burglar's tools ? ' asked Peter, patting the closed case.

'What d'you mean ? ' asked the policeman.

'Dad got his attaché case swopped in the bus this morning. Look what was in the one that was left.' He opened the lid and the visitor peered inside.

'Oh,' he said calmly, 'that'll be the locksmith's case that was reported missing this forenoon. He *was* mad—turning up to open a woman's door with only a flask and a few sandwiches ! '

Seeing signs of another fainting attack, Maisie went for a glass of water while Willie, forgetting his hunger, urged the policeman to sit down and give him his ' crack,' adding, 'Hoo's yer faither noo that he hasnae the Home Guard tae play cairds at ? '

Rejecting the seat, the young fellow admitted that his father's health was good but, as he was in a hurry, would they please let him know how many tickets they wanted for the concert.

Sarah's voice rang firm with relief : ' We'll take six ! '

'But there's only four of us ! ' protested Maisie.

'I know, but I'll want two extra for the M'Corduroys. I'm so grateful ! ' Then she suddenly had a genuine fainting fit. When she had revived both policeman and locksmith's tools were gone ; only the six tickets remained as evidence of her ordeal.

CHAPTER 10

PETER'S GIRL FRIEND

FROM time to time Maisie would be allowed the exclusive use of the sitting-room for the purpose of entertaining her friends, male and female ; but it was something of a surprise to Sarah when Peter, newly turned twenty, suddenly announced that he was intending bringing a girl friend to the house one evening. Intrigued, Sarah made up her mind to be hospitable. She was therefore indignant, when the selected evening arrived, to find that Maisie was not similarly disposed.

'Where are you going with that towel ? ' Sarah demanded.

'To wash my hair,' was the girl's casual answer.

'Oh, not tonight, Maisie. And Peter's girl coming up.'

'I don't see why I shouldn't wash my hair ! We don't want to give her the impression that we're all het-up about her visit ! '

Said Sarah : 'But I've lit the sitting-room fire. And I've tried to make everything nice for her coming——'

From the fireside came Willie's contribution to Sarah's vexation : 'If Maisie's gonnae wash 'er hair, Ah suppose Ah'll can get sittin' in ma shirt sleeves ? '

'I'll shirt-sleeves-you ! As for you, Maisie, it's too bad of you to carry on like this ! When I think of how fussy you are when any of your boy friends come to the house——'

'Oh, but that's different,' retorted Maisie. 'You must admit they've all had some refinement about them. Not like this cutie of Peter's.'

'Well, all the more reason for letting her see how well Peter's been brought up ! '

'But if nane o' yez has met the lassie,' protested Willie, ' Ah don't see hoo yez can say whit she's like ! '

'She's a niece of Mrs McTweed's and that's enough,' said Maisie.

'Whit ! Mrs McTweed that used tae bide doon ablow us ?' asked Willie, as though he had not unpleasant memories.

'The same,' said Maisie, making great play with her towel.

'Guid auld Mrs McTweed ! D'ye mind, Serah, when we flittit intae that hoose she came up greetin' that 'er man wis a baker an' couldnae get sleepin' fur us-yins ham-ham-hammerin' ?'

'I remember all right,' said Sarah ; 'but I'll say this much for Mrs McTweed—she was a hard-working wee buddy and——'

'Ye're right, Ah'm sayin' ye're right,' interposed Maisie in imitation of the repetitive Mrs McTweed.

'And if this niece of hers is anything like her,' went on Sarah, unheeding the interruption, 'she'll make a good wife for Peter.'

'Good grief, Mother,' exclaimed Maisie. 'They're not even engaged yet—and considering Peter's tender age——'

Her speech was cut short by the entrance of the youth in question, who somewhat self-consciously announced that he was on his way to meet Ivy to bring her to the house.

'Ivy !' Maisie's tones were derisive. 'What a name !' She then burst into song to the effect that mares eat oats and does eat oats but little lambs eat ivy. Her special emphasis on the diet of the last-mentioned group of animals brought forth her brother's angry snarl :

'You shut up ! I'm fed to the teeth with you ! Treating the girl like the dirt beneath your feet.'

'I never said a word,' replied Maisie.

'Maybe not, but you looked ugly enough when you were singing.'

Since compliments were thus flying, Willie felt compelled to wing a few of his own. 'Maisie cannae help lookin' ugly,' he observed. 'Ah'm aye tellin' 'er it's no' a powder puff hur face needs, it's a powder magazine.'

'Is that so ?' remarked Maisie, determined to get her own back. 'Well, everybody tells me I get more like my father every day !'

'Oh, be quiet—all of you!' said Sarah. Turning to Peter, she went on, 'Peter, son, I wish we knew a wee bit more about this girl. Could you not tell us something?'

'That's right,' put in Willie. 'Sit doon there an' tell us whit size o' shoes she takes.'

Sulkily, Peter refused to oblige, adding that he had a good mind to tell the girl not to come at all.

This suggestion horrified his mother. 'Oh, you can't do that, Peter, after all the preparations I've made. We're having fish custard for supper—a thing we haven't been able to have for ages. And the sitting-room fire's on. Only—it's kind of queer not knowing anything about the girl.'

Softened by his mother's earnestness, the lad asked, 'What do you want me to tell you, then? You can't expect me to start and rave about her when Maisie's standing there waiting to make a fool of me.'

'I can't make a fool of you, Peter,' was Maisie's reply. 'Nature's done that already.'

'Oh, can you not be original for once in your life!' snapped Peter.

Reproof in her tone and manner, Sarah said, 'That was a terrible thing to say, Maisie!'—but Peter, ungrateful for her moral support, turned on his mother and said:

'You shut up Mother! I can stick up for myself!'—a remark that in turn brought Willie into the arena with:

'Peter! Don't you talk like that tae yer mother or Ah'll take ma haun' affa your jaw.'

'I'd like to see you trying it!' said Peter.

Sarah wailed, 'Oh, this is terrible! It doesn't promise very well for the girl when she's causing a family row before she's even seen us. Sit down, Willie. The boy's excited—he doesn't know what he's saying.'

'But I'm not a boy!' yelled Peter. 'That's what makes me see red! You're all treating me as if I was ten instead of twenty. Look here, Mother, I'm sorry for narking you just now—it's just that I feel you're all—well, sort of up against Ivy before you've even seen her. And I want you to like her and her to like you.

Oh, maybe I *am* a bit excited!' He broke off. 'I don't know what I'm saying.'

Maisie, in a particularly waspish mood, murmured, 'You're telling me!'

For a moment the lad hesitated, then plunged into speech again. 'Maisie, listen! I know you can't help trying to take me down a peg every time you open your mouth—but please—could you not pretend—just for tonight?' The girl's only response was to flick her towel over the furniture, so Peter continued, 'Please, Maisie. You can rag me as much as you like afterwards.'

'Okay, big boy,' said Maisie grudgingly. 'I mean okay, big man.'

'Oh, you're hopeless!' Turning to his father he went on, 'And Dad—would *you* do something for me too?'

'Whit?'

'Could you—I mean—ugh, I don't know how to put it, but do you think you could kind of try to, well—speak more like a foreman? You see——'

At that, Maisie dropped her offensive manner and said, 'Good luck to you, Peter. I've tried till I'm blue in the face.'

Instantly Willie was adopting his defensive manner. 'Whit's up wi' the wey Ah speak? Ah'm sure everybody kens whit Ah'm meanin' fur tae be at! Whit mair d'ye want?'

All of them protesting simultaneously, the man got no detailed idea of their objections, but the general impression was such that he shouted them down with : 'Ach, Ah wid be like a coo wi' a gun tryin' tae speak Pan Loaf. Ah'd 'a been faur better tae've went oot the nicht an' ye coulda kidded the lassie on ye were a' dukes an' duchesses!'

'My goodness, Dad's in the huff!' said Maisie.

'Ah'm no' in the huff!' roared Willie; 'but Ah'm sick tae daith aye bein' jumped on fur the wey Ah speak!'

Glancing at the clock, Peter gulped out that he would need to hurry so as not to keep Ivy waiting; his hand on the door-knob, he addressed his mother :

'I say, do you think *you* could do something for me too, Mother?'

Sarah gaped at her son. ' What ? Me ? Why, what's wrong with me ? I'm sure *I* try to speak proper ! '

' It's not that, Mother. It's—it's yon photo of me in my birthday suit lying on a cushion.'

' What about it ? I think it's a lovely picture, that ! '

' Well—*please*, Mother, will you *not* show it to Ivy ? '

' Why not ? '

Before Peter could elaborate the obvious, his father nipped in with : ' Ah'm sure the lassie should be real pleased tae see sich a lot o' ye ! '

' Willie ! ' snapped Sarah. ' Don't be vulgar ! '

' Come on, Mother. Say you won't show it to Ivy ! ' pleaded Peter from the door.

' Oh, all right,' was the resigned response. ' But all the same——'

' There's just one thing more,' said Peter.

Maisie folded up her towel, saying, ' Heavens, Peter, you've had a whack at us all. There's nobody left to give instructions to.'

' This is for the lot of you ! ' Peter flung over his shoulder. ' I want you to clear out of the sitting-room and let me have a chat with Ivy.' He slammed the door.

' Jeengs, is he gonnae ask 'er fur the len' o' money ? ' asked Willie. ' He's ower young tae marry yet,' he added tunefully.

But Sarah had no ear for her husband's little song. ' Did you ever hear the like of that ? ' she demanded. ' Turning round and telling his mother what she should and what she shouldn't do ! And me so proud of that photo too ! '

' What about the rest of us ? ' asked Maisie.

' Ay, we a' catched it the nicht,' said Willie.

' Oh, but that was different ! ' Sarah looked around for something upon which to vent her sore feelings. ' Put away that towel, Maisie,' she ordered, ' and come and help me to finish the setting of this table, and then we can get into the sitting-room and be ready for the girl coming.' Her annoyance faded away as she hustled and bustled ; indeed her activity, both vocal and pedestrian, was so great that her husband was moved to protest.

'Ach, Serah, can we no' jist cairry on the wey we always dae ? Whit's the use o' kiddin' on in front o' the lassie ? '

His only answer was the flinging of his jacket into his lap, with instructions to put it on and keep his mouth shut. There was a muttered postscript about behaviour suitable to a foreman, but the man did not trouble to inquire too closely for what he was not anxious to learn. In any case Sarah had changed the subject and was giving him instructions about serving the fish custard. He shuffled his shoulders into his jacket with only half his mind on what was being said to him.

Ten minutes later the three of them were sitting in state awaiting the arrival of Peter with his girl friend. Willie's spirits had been restored, so that he suggested amiably that Maisie might fill in the waiting time with what he called ' a choon on the pianna.'

' Yes, go on ! ' urged Sarah. ' It's a shame the way you never touch that piano after all the money that was spent on lessons for you.'

' Two whole quarters ! ' sneered Maisie.

' Two quarters ! ' exclaimed Sarah. ' It was more like two years ! Everybody used to say you had a lovely touch ! '

' A lovely touch ! ' The sneer was still in evidence. ' What an expression ! I wonder, Mother, when you and Dad will realise that I can play just well enough to know I can't play at all ! '

' Havers,' said Willie, missing the point. ' Ye can surely gi'e us " The Sailor's Shirt." '

Maisie sniffed, and for a moment or two there was silence, which was eventually broken by Sarah's saying, ' My, I wonder if the girl's excited at coming to see Peter's relations ? Willie— do you remember the state I was in the first time you took me to see your folks ? '

' Fine Ah mind it ! It wis the only time in yer life ye had nothin' tae say.'

' You weren't much better yourself—sitting like a knotless thread.' Sarah giggled as her mind dwelt further on the occasion now almost forgotten : ' And d'you remember your mother couldn't talk about anything but the weather ? '

Maisie decided it was time to change the subject. 'You two,' she said, 'are taking this visit tonight far too seriously. Girls nowadays are so casual——'

But Sarah was not listening; her ears, instead, were strained to catch sounds from outside the room. 'Shsh!' she said, interrupting her daughter's dissertation on the mental attitude of the modern girl; 'here they are. Is my hair all right?'

'Yes,' said Maisie. 'Now, remember, Mother, don't say: "Pleased to meet you." Say: "How d'you do."'

'Oh, stop checking me,' snapped Sarah as the door opened and Peter pushed a girl into the room, saying:

'Here we are.'

Sarah stepped forward, holding out her hand. 'Oh, come away in. You'll be Ivy. How d'you do.'

'Fine, thanks,' said Ivy, shifting a piece of chewing-gum from one side of her mouth to the other. 'How yerself?'

'This is Dad, Ivy,' said Peter.

Shaking hands, Willie started out to say, 'Hoo'ye,' but corrected himself and said with great care, 'How do you do.'

'Pleased to meet ye,' said Ivy, who obviously had no sister to guide her.

Peter, determined to adopt a style of introduction he had heard Ivy use, brought the two girls face to face and said, 'This is a Miss McTweed to a Miss McFlannel.'

'How d'you do,' was Maisie's rather stiff acknowledgment.

'Pleased to meet ye,' was Ivy's.

'Won't you take off your coat?' asked Sarah. 'Peter can hang it on the hallstand for you.'

'Okeydoke,' said the visitor.

Sarah took the coat that was handed to her and said, 'It hasn't been so cold lately, has it?'

'I never noticed,' said the girl.

'Come on an' sit doon at the fire here!' The invitation came from Willie who added, 'Unless ye're feart ye gi'e yersel' tartan legs.'

Passing the coat over to Peter who went to hang it as instructed, Sarah threw a warning look in the direction of her husband, but

Willie preferred to answer the girl's question as to the meaning of 'tartan legs.'

'Ach,' said Willie, 'lassie's legs that's a' mottled wi' sittin' too near the fire.'

The next few moments were occupied finding seating accommodation round the fireside, Ivy preferring to sit well back, presumably in the interests of her legs, but when conversation seemed reluctant to start up again Sarah plunged once more into a statement about the weather. Unfortunately it was a direct contradiction of her earlier expression of opinion, for this time she insisted that the weather was cold for the time of the year. No-one making any comment she went on, 'Was it raining when you came in, Peter?'

'No.' His monosyllable fell like a stone into a bottomless quarry.

At length Maisie decided to take a hand. 'Are you fond of reading, Ivy?' she asked.

'Me?' queried the visitor. 'No. I havenae the time.'

Thus silenced, Maisie retired from the field of endeavour, and once more the party gazed into the heart of the fire.

Suddenly Willie eased his collar from his neck, complained of the heat of the room, and asked Maisie if she would give them a 'choon on the pianna.' This Maisie declined to do, suggesting that Peter might, instead, give the company a tune on his violin.

Ivy's jaws stopped working. Slapping Peter on the back she squawked, 'The wee smasher! Ye never told me ye could play the fiddle, Pete.'

'Ugh, forget it,' said Peter in great self-consciousness.

'Do you play anything?' inquired Maisie politely.

'Ay—beebawbabbity,' replied Ivy with a raucous laugh.

Once again there was silence which was broken eventually by a significant cough from Peter. Misunderstanding its meaning, Sarah at first commiserated with her son on having fallen a victim to the common cold, but something in the expression of his face reminded her of his request to have the exclusive use of the room so that he might have Ivy's undiluted company. This she was glad to give him, her powers of conversation being at an end and her dislike of the girl being excessive. The visitor's chewing-gum, as well as her manner, her overdone make-up, her scarlet finger-nails, combined to rouse Sarah's old-fashioned prejudices.

She rose. ' Maisie, I think you and I should go and make the supper ready,' she said. ' Coming, Willie ? '

' Naw. Ah'm fine here ! ' Willie settled himself more comfortably in his chair. ' Gi'es a shout when ye're ready.'

' But Willie——'

' Whit are ye pintin' at ? ' he demanded gawkily.

' Come on, Dad,' said Maisie from the door. ' Come on and chop sticks for the fire in the morning.'

' Ach, Ah can dae that efter.'

' Willie ! I *want* you to come.' Clearly, it was a case for plain speaking, thought Sarah.

Something in her manner made the man rise with a grunt, and say, ' Oh, all right. Onythin' fur a quiet wife.'

When the door had closed on the retreating forces, Ivy murmured, ' Poor sap ! '

' Who's a poor sap ? ' asked Peter, changing his seat so as to be nearer his guest.

' Your old man. Like a wee puppy dog.' She gave a whistle more suited to a hillside than to a polite parlour, then, in gruff herd-like tones, she growled, ' Come in ahint, min ! '

Peter was indignant and was about to defend his father when Ivy shouted him down : ' You fairly kidded me on about yer father. I thought ye said he was a foreman.'

' So he is ! '

' And talks like thon ? If Maisie's a teacher, can she not learn him to speak proper ? '

Appalled at this unexpected and forthright attack, Peter could only make gestures of protest as Ivy went on :

' I suppose Maisie'll be too busy readin' books for to waste time on 'er old man ! ' Once again she indulged in some mimicry. ' Are you fahnd of reading ? ' she smirked in imitation of Maisie's earlier attempt at conversation.

' Here, Ivy——'

' As for yer mother—all she can talk about is the weather.'

'Ivy, listen to me! Dad left the room because I'd told them I wanted a wee while alone with you!'

'Oh yeah?' Once again the chewing-gum changed molars.

'But I'm not sure now whether I want to,' continued Peter sulkily.

'How?'

'Well, for one thing, I don't like to hear my folk being laughed at the way you've done just now.'

'But, ye gods, I couldnae help laughin' at them! Your Dad sittin' there a' dressed up in 'is jaiket——'

'You shut up about my Dad! He's worth a hundred of you!' Peter's romantic notions were suffering a rude shock.

'Oh yeah?' taunted Ivy. 'And I suppose yer mother'll be worth a thousand of me with her Sunday beads on!'

Peter gaped, then said ruefully, 'Oh, Ivy, what's come over you? You've changed so much I hardly know you!'

'Me changed? I like that! It's *you* that's changed! I thought you were the cat's pyjamas till I seen ye in the bosom of yer fam'ly the now. Huh—ye're nothin' but yer mammy's wee tumpshy. I bet she's got a photo of you somewhere that she takes out and kisses—you lying in your bare skuddy on a cushion.'

Aghast, Peter demanded to know who had told her.

Taking this to be an admission, Ivy shrieked in triumph, 'I knew it! I jist knew it! She's the type a'right.'

'You shut up about my mother!'

'As for Maisie——'

'Here!' Peter got to his feet. 'I'm not going to listen to you miscalling my family.'

'Nobody's asking you to!' was the cool retort. 'Are ye sure ye wouldnae like to go an' help yer mammy wi' the supper?'

'Ivy!' There was reproach in the tones. 'I never heard you talk like this before. You—you're not the same girl!'

'And you're not the same chap. You didn't half kid me on about the toffs ye were.'

'I did not!'

'You did sot!' Ivy was on her feet now too. 'I never thought you lived up a close in a two-room-and-kitchen.'

'It's a three-room-and-kitchen!'

'So what! I was expectin' a butler or somethin' to open the door to us.'

Once again Peter said reproachfully, 'Oh, Ivy!'

'Ach, quit the "Oh, Ivy!" stunt. Where's my coat? I wanna go home.'

'What! Are you not going to wait for supper? After all the trouble Mother has taken——'

'Ach, you and yer mother!'

'But, Ivy, you can't go! It wouldn't be polite. After all——'

'Polite? What do I care about politeness? You get me my coat. You had an awful nerve, so you had, invitin' me up to meet suchna bunch o' stuffed birds——'

'Here—that'll do! I'll get you your coat!' He opened the door.

'Okay, big boy. Suits me. I'll not ask you to get it for me again—ever. I was beginnin' to think you were too narrow-minded for me anyway.'

Peter dived into the dimness of the lobby, brought back the coat and held it spread for the girl to poke her arms into the sleeves. 'I'll see you home,' he said miserably.

'Don't bother yer bonnet—I'll see maself home. It's too late for wee boys like you to be away from their mammies. Where's my bag?'

He handed her the overcrowded article indicated and wondered what had become of the one he had given her the previous Christmas.

'So long,' said Ivy, making great play with her jaws. 'I've had a lucky escape.'

'Not as lucky as me,' said Peter. 'You're nothing but a wee gold-digger. Take what you can get out of a chap——'

'So what! A girl wants a good time, does she not?' was the unruffled retort. They moved towards the outside door. 'Tell yer mother I'm sorry to miss the fish custard.'

'Fish custard?' gulped Peter. 'How did you know?'

'Ach—this is a fish-custard fam'ly!' Leaving the astounded Peter gaping, Ivy opened the door, went out and clattered down the stairs in her high-heeled shoes. In a state of shock, Peter closed the door and went to the kitchen.

'Hallo, Peter,' said his mother when she saw him. 'We'll not be a minute. I think you could tell Ivy to come.'

Peter closed the kitchen door after him, saying heavily, 'She won't be coming.'

'What?' asked Sarah, pausing in the act of pouring boiling water on to tea-leaves.

'Don't tell me she's gone home to change the colour of her toe-nails,' said Maisie superciliously.

As for Willie, he stared at his bewildered son. 'Whit's up?' he asked kindly.

'She's away,' said the lad. 'She'll not be back. Ever.'

'Cheers!' roared Willie. 'Ah'll can take aff ma jaiket.' As proof of this ability, he not only extricated himself from his sartorial bonds as far as the jacket was concerned, but he took off his collar and tie as well. Sarah, for her part, was too taken up with her duties as hostess to protest.

'Peter—don't say she's away without getting her supper or saying goodnight or anything.'

'She's away,' was all Peter could bring himself to say.

'Have you had a row?' asked Maisie.

'Something of the kind.'

Sarah put down the kettle and the teapot. 'This is terrible. And the fish custard done to a turn too! What did you quarrel about?'

'Oh—things.'

'She's not your type, Peter!' said Maisie in a tone that was, for her, very affectionate. 'I can't think what you saw in her. She's good-looking, of course, in a flashy sort of way, but she's cheap!'

Sarah added her opinions, saying quite frankly that she was glad, that the girl frightened her. 'Never mind, son,' she went on, patting his shoulder comfortingly, 'there's as many good fish in the sea as ever came out of it.'

'Speakin' aboot fish,' put in Willie quickly; 'whit aboot that fish custard? Ah could eat twa helpin's.'

'I don't want any,' said Peter.

'Cheers!' said his father. 'That'll be three helpin's—ma ain an' Ivy's an' yours.'

Maisie looked at her doleful brother. 'Come on, Peter. Snap out of it! If you're honest with yourself you'll admit you're really quite pleased.'

'I—suppose—I—am!' he admitted unwillingly.

Willie drew his chair closer to the table. 'Come on, folks. Muck in! Ah could eat ma wey through a knacker's midden.'

'Willie!' Sarah protested. 'If you'd said that when Ivy was here, I'd 've blamed you for being the cause of the split between her and Peter.' She turned to her son, saying, 'By the way—*was* it because of the way your father speaks?'

'No,' answered the lad with mental reservations.

Maisie shrugged her shoulders, saying, 'Well, I'm sure I did my little best to be agreeable. Did I say something I didn't ought'er?'

With more mental reservations, Peter said 'No' once again.

'Then it must've been me,' said Sarah. 'Did I talk about the weather?'

As before, Peter said 'No.'

'Then what was it?' continued the rejected mother-in-law-elect.

'She—she called me a mammy's tumpshy.' Peter gazed at the others defying them to laugh at him. 'I couldn't stand for that!'

No-one making any comment on this, Sarah returned to the scullery and her tea-making job; Maisie took the fish custard from the oven and placed it on the table, done to an appetising turn. Peter felt the aroma through his wounded susceptibilities.

'That fish custard looks not too bad,' he observed.

'It's wizard,' said Maisie. 'I'll serve it out and save Dad the bother.'

Willie could not be expected to object to this usurpation of his duties as head of the house; Peter watched the spoonfuls of fish being put on the several plates, then he found his voice once again.

'I say, Maisie—doing anything tonight?'

'No—why?'

'I was wondering if we'd slip out and see a flick.'

In astonishment, Maisie stopped, spoon in hand : 'Jolly good idea.   Have I to bring my purse?'

'No.   I'll pay the damage—sort of thank-offering, if you like.' Then, as she went on ladling an overdose on to his father's plate, Peter shouted, 'Oy!   You're giving Dad more fish than me.'

In the scullery Sarah smiled.   It was all right.   It couldn't have been love—his stomach was still in order!

CHAPTER 11

POISON—IVY

BUT they were not completely rid of the unpleasant Ivy, as Maisie found one day some weeks later when she encountered the damsel on a bus.

'Hallo, Maisie,' said Ivy, sitting down beside her with the imperturbability of her type.

'Good evening,' was Maisie's cool response.

'The bus is awful crowded, isn't it?'

'Is it?'

'I don't think you remember me. I used to be goin'-set wi' your brother Peter. I was up at your house, mind? Miss McTweed's the name.'

'I remember you perfectly,' said Maisie.

'How's Peter gettin' on these days?'

'Quite well, thank you.'

'It's funny meetin' you like this,' went on the irrepressible Ivy. 'I was thinkin' of comin' up for to see Peter the night.'

Maisie's 'Oh?' was not very encouraging but notwithstanding Ivy continued:

'Uhha.'

There was a cocksureness that was faintly disturbing; Maisie felt the balloon of this self-assurance ought to be pricked. She racked her brains for an idea and to her discredit it must be admitted that she had to fall back on inaccuracy.

'Peter's going with another girl now, you know.'

'Is 'e? I've never saw him along with her, well.'

'Oh, she doesn't live in Glasgow. They only see one another when she comes south to sing at concerts. She lives in Drumforber.' Maisie watched her companion's face closely but there seemed no untoward reaction.

'Huh—musical, is she? She must be tickled pink when Peter plays 'is fiddle. Are they goin'-set?'

'Are they what?' asked Maisie, although she knew perfectly well the meaning of the phrase.

'Crickey, you're on the shelf a'right if ye don't know what "goin'-set" means,' was the cheeky retort. 'I mean—are they engaged or jist winchin'?'

'They're not engaged as far as I know. But I can tell you this much—it's no use you trying to get Peter into your toils again—you managed to sicken him pretty thoroughly.'

'D'ye tell me that?' jeered Ivy. 'Well, 'is collie-wobbles'll be a bit more upset by the time I'm done with 'im the night.'

'What do you mean?'

'Oh, jist you wait and I'll show ye, as the passenger said to the boat steward when he told him he couldn't be sick in the saloon.'

'I think you're perfectly disgusting,' said Maisie, turning up her nose. 'And anyway, I'm afraid it won't be convenient for you to call tonight. We—um—we're expecting other visitors.'

'Och, they'll no' bother me!'

'Besides, I'm not sure that Peter will be at home himself.'

'Don't you kid yourself!' said Ivy with a raucous laugh; 'if you're havin' visitors, Peter'll have to be on the spot—the big mammy's tumpshy.'

Maisie tried to wither the girl with a look but was not successful. 'If you feel like that about him, why do you want to see him tonight?'

'Ye'd like to know, would ye no'?' taunted Ivy.

'Well, he's my brother.'

'Huh—some brother. Ye must be real proud of 'im!'

Something both in Ivy's manner and in her sneering tones made Maisie uneasy, but she persisted in her own aloof bearing as she said:

'I couldn't expect you to appreciate him.'

'Appreciate him? Ye don't appreciate chaps like your Peter —ye stick them on yer chest when ye've a cold!' She rose, saying, 'I see there's a seat beside my pal at the back. I'll away the now. I'll be seein' ye.'

Maisie turned on her sharply. 'But I'm telling you—you're wasting your time if you're trying to make it up with Peter.'

'Jist you wait !' tossed back Ivy, not caring who heard her. 'By the time I'm done with your Peter the night, he'll be glad to make it up with me . . . unless he'd rather go to the court.'

'Cuc—court ?' stammered Maisie.

'You heard me ! So long. Tell yer mother to be sure an' wear 'er apron. She'll need it for cryin' into.'

'You little beast !' stormed Maisie. 'What are you hinting at ?'

But, without giving any further details, Ivy waved gaily and went to the back of the bus, and by the time it had reached Maisie's stopping-place, Ivy had disappeared. Maisie raced home, her heart-beats hurrying like her footsteps. She burst into the house, shouting, 'Mother ! Mother ! Where are you ?'

'In the kitchen,' came the reassuring reply.

'Oh, Mother,' panted Maisie without preliminaries, 'you remember Ivy McTweed ?'

'Yes—a right cheeky bizzum, she was.'

'I met her in the bus just now. She's coming up tonight to see Peter.'

'What about ?'

'She wouldn't tell me, but she hinted at something . . .' Maisie searched for the most tactful words, 'something disgraceful. Oh, Mother !'

Sarah flopped into a chair, fumbling with her neckband. 'What on earth can it be ?' Her mind leapt to the worst situation with unfailing promptitude : 'She's not going to have a—I mean—oh, Maisie, it can't be *that* !'

Fully realising what her mother meant by *that*, Maisie did nothing to dispel her fears when she merely explained that Ivy had said something about Peter perhaps having to go to court.

'Oh dear-dear, this is dreadful !' gasped Sarah. 'Tell your father to come here—he's in the sitting-room.'

Maisie fetched her father by the remote-control method of shouting for him. Willie hurried to the scene of dismay complaining that he had been interrupted in the task of giving the dog a few piano lessons, and hoped, therefore, that his presence had not been demanded unnecessarily.

'Oh, Willie,' said Sarah from the depths of her handkerchief, 'Peter's gone and got himself into trouble with Ivy McTweed.' Then, overcome with self-pity which she tried to pass off as embarrassment, she added, 'Maisie—you tell him what she said.'

'I met her in the bus just now. She's coming up to see Peter tonight. I tried to put her off by telling her we were having visitors.'

As might have been expected, Willie felt entitled to a little self-pity on his own account. 'Whit !' he exclaimed. 'Visitors the night ? Ach, Serah, can we never get the hoose tae wursels ? Ah wis wantin' tae listen tae a wee play on the wireless.'

'Willie ! How can you talk about wee plays and us with a calamity like this on our hands.'

'Whit calamity ?'

'Ivy McTweed !'

'Wha's she when she's at hame ?'

'Peter's girl friend !' put in Maisie, since her mother was so infuriated by the man's pseudo-stupidity that she could not form words. 'D'you not remember she was here one night ?'

'But Ah thocht Peter wis kinna sweet on a wee lassie he met in Drumforber ?'

'He's been sweet on half a dozen girls since then !' Maisie too was beginning to lose patience with the man. 'But he *used* to go with Ivy McTweed !'

'An' is she suin' 'im fur breach o' promise ?'

Sarah sniffled softly into her handkerchief, allowing Maisie to continue with the explanations. 'It's got something to do with the court anyway, Dad. I say—could we not get Peter out of the road for a bit ?'

'You mean—send him abroad ?' The query came in muffled tones from Sarah.

'Ach !' declared Willie, 'this is gettin' beyond me. First ye scare the life oota me by sayin' we're haein' visitors the night, then ye burst intae somethin' aboot the lassie McTweed—an' noo ye're haverin' aboot Peter goin' abroad.'

'Willie! Don't *try* to be stupid! We're only wanting to help Peter!' Turning to Maisie, she said, 'We simply must think of something. Could he go away for a holiday, d'you think?'

'There ye go again!' said Willie. 'Jumpin' aboot like fleas in a model. Nae wonder Ah cannae follow ye! Ah'm away ben the hoose again!' He was in the act of turning on his heel when his wife stopped him.

'Willie—you'll just stay here and help us with your advice!'

'It's no' advice you're wantin', Serah,' retorted Willie. 'It's jist somebody tae say Ay-ay tae ye. If Peter wants tae marry this lassie McTweed, it's his business, no' oors.'

'But Peter doesn't want to marry her, Dad!' pointed out Maisie.

'And anyway,' came the observation from Sarah, whose tears had been dried by indignation, 'I don't want her for a daughter-in-law! Not at any price. We'll need to try and buy her off.'

'Peter always said she was a gold-digger,' said Maisie.

Overcome by the thought of the enormity of her son's plight, Sarah retired once again behind her handkerchief and wailed, 'Oh, my poor wee Peter!'—an attitude that roused her husband's contempt.

'Away wi' ye! He's five-foot-ten, an' got a' 'is ain teeth!'

'I tell you what, Maisie,' said Sarah, emerging once more; 'when that girl comes up tonight we'll make Peter go to bed and we'll tell her she can't see him, and you and I will deal with her.'

At that there was a distant banging of the outer door, a cheery whistle which, though tuneless, was significant enough in that it heralded Peter. He did not have time to greet the family before his mother descended upon him with all the flutter of a concerned hen for her chick.

'Oh, Peter, my own wee Peter! Come and tell your mother all about it!'

Peter gaped. 'About what? The lecture I've been at?'

To hide his emotion at such a tender scene, Willie barked out gruffly that this was a fine how-dy-do.

Once again Peter gaped, tried to uncoil his mother's arms from his neck, and asked the reason for this sudden display of affection.

'Never you mind the girl,' said Sarah, patting him on one shoulder ; '*we*'ll all stick by you, no matter what she says. Just you get to bed right away.'

'Get to bed ? ' repeated the young fellow in amazement. ' Maisie—can you give me the low-down on this ? '

'Ivy McTweed's on your track. She seems to have some hold over you,' said Maisie obligingly.

'What the . . .' began Peter, breaking off to complain that his mother's love was robbing him of breath.

'I can't help it, Peter,' sobbed Sarah ; 'it's terrible to think of you being in the clutches of that awful girl ! '

'You're the only girl I'm in the clutches of at the moment, Mother. Let go a sec', and tell me what all this is in aid of.'

Self-pity disguised as self-consciousness made Sarah answer, ' Oh, Peter, I can't bring myself to speak about such things. But never mind—we'll buy her off.'

'Listen, Mother,' said Peter firmly, 'I haven't the foggiest notion of what you're driving at. Supposing you tell me in words of one syllable ? '

Instantly there was a polysyllabic explanation coming from three directions ; holding up his hand for silence, Peter asked Maisie for her version. Her effort was as nearly monosyllabic as she could make it.

'I met the girl in the bus on my way home just now. She told me she's coming up here to see you—about—well . . . *you* should know ! '

'Oh dear, the disgrace of it all,' wailed Sarah. 'I never thought I would live to see this day. Oh, Peter——'

'Mother,' Peter was getting exasperated, 'what the heck are you raving about ? I've done nothing I need to be ashamed of ! '

'Then why is she talking about taking you to court ? ' demanded his mother.

'Court ? What court ? '

Maisie was left to complete the innuendo. 'Well, we thought—um—you know . . . it was a case of . . . oh, to hang, I can't put it into words ! '

'For heaven's sake, Maisie,' stormed Peter, 'will you tell me what's up ? Either you've got a dirty mind, or I have. Come on, out with it.'

' Oh dear, this is terrible ! ' wailed Sarah all over again, while Willie made for the door declaring that this was no place for him. He intimated that he intended resuming his interrupted instructions to the dog on the art and craft of piano playing.

'Dad, for the luva mike, don't desert me ! ' pleaded Peter ; ' this pair have got a kink in their brain. Listen, Mother—I've got an absolutely clear conscience as far as Ivy or any other girl is concerned——'

At that moment the doorbell rang. 'That'll be her ! ' exclaimed Sarah. ' Peter, son—away you to your bed ! '

' I'm going ! ' was the promising announcement, which was immediately followed by a disappointing qualification, '. . . to the door ! '

' I think you should let Mother and me handle this,' said Maisie, laying a restraining hand on her brother. ' You're much too innocent to be——'

' Let me alone ! ' Peter shrugged himself free and left the kitchen.

Willie scratched his head. 'Ah wish Ah knew whit a' this wis aboot.' He sat down in his usual chair at the fireside and gazed dumbly at his wife who paced up and down in an agony of increasing self-pity and decreasing self-control, the remaining shreds of the last-mentioned being almost torn from her when she heard Peter's voice in the distance welcoming, not Ivy, but his Uncle Mattha.

' Oh ! ' she almost screamed, ' as if we hadn't enough trouble on our hands without that man butting in ! '

Willie, on the other hand, welcomed his brother cordially as light relief from the unintelligible gloom that had surrounded the household for the past few minutes. ' Hoo'ye, Mattha ! ' he hailed the visitor. ' Hoo's yer corns the night ? '

' No' sae bad,' was the reluctant admission. ' Ah've gotten a new corn cure wi' castor ile in it. It's an awful smell, but.'

Under cover of the somewhat cold greeting between Mattha and his sister-in-law, Maisie whispered to Peter that she wouldn't have thought their uncle would have been conscious of any unpleasantness more than usual emanating from his feet.

' Sit doon, man,' urged Willie, ' an' take aff yer bunnet.'

' Ach, it's no' worth ma while takin' it aff. Ah'm no' bidin' that long.'

' We're expecting a visitor, Mattha.' Sarah's tones conveyed several shades of meaning ranging from reproof to dismissal.

' Och, don't fash yersel' aboot me,' was the calm retort, ' Ah'm used wi' meetin' folk.'

' But this is something extra private ! '

' Imagine that ! ' The adenoidal ejaculation, like Sarah's earlier remark, ranged over a wide area of meaning, from surprise to downright disbelief. Turning to his brother, Mattha continued in complete unconcern, ' Ah jist came up fur tae ask ye, Wullie, if ye'd gi'e me a haun' wi' the paperin' o' oor room. Ye tellt me tae slabber the paste on tae the back o' the wallpaper an' then fold it back on itsel'. Well, Ah musta left it ower lang, for a' the paper's stuck thegither that hard Ah cannae get it lowsed.'

' Ach, man, ye didnae dae a' the paper at wance, did ye ? '

' Wis that no' whit ye tellt me tae dae ? '

Willie's heated denial was interrupted by the ringing of the doorbell. ' Willie,' said Sarah with emphasis, ' that'll be Ivy McTweed now. What about you going out with Mattha ? You could finish your discussion outside—or I tell you what— just you away home with him and help him with his wallpaper.' Her husband refusing to co-operate, she had to turn her attentions in the direction of her son who was even now moving towards the outer door. There was something of a tussle at the kitchen door, Sarah finally yielding to Peter's superior knowledge of manhandling. She found herself dumped in a chair and being told to keep out of business that did not immediately pertain to her. Never before having received treatment like this at the hands of her son, the woman could only gape as he left the kitchen followed by Maisie.

' I say, Peter, wait for me ! ' whispered Maisie when the kitchen door was shut and they were alone in the lobby. ' Peter

—before you open the door I—I . . . oh, to blazes, I don't know how to put it, but—I'm on your side. If you're needing help—money or anything—you can count on me ! '

This was such a completely new and unexpected evidence of sisterly affection that Peter could only blurt out, ' You're a humdinger, Maisie, but I don't think I'll need help. Now, away you go back to the kitchen.' His tones were brusque ; he realised that himself, so he called her back. ' I say, Maisie . . .'

' Uhha ? ' For her part Maisie was now ashamed of the show of feeling she had displayed.

' Do you—really mean—all that ? ' stammered Peter.

' Of course I do ! I'll back you up till your nose bleeds ! '

With that she was gone, leaving him to open the door and cope with the situation himself.

' Oh, it's you, Ivy,' he said a moment later, viewing the pert figure on the doormat.

' Yep, it's me. Ye don't look awful pleased to see me ! '

' Why should I ? ' Even Sarah could not have found anything to worry about in the coolness of his manner.

' Are ye not goin' to invite me in ? '

' Nope.'

' Well, I've came up to have a private talk with you.' She raised her voice. ' Maybe ye don't mind the neighbours hearin' all about yer affairs ? '

' I haven't got any private affairs to talk about with you.'

' Oh, have ye not ? ' The tones were louder still. ' That's what *you* think. You that always prides yerself on bein' sichna gentleman—keepin' a lady standin' on yer doormat.'

Peter looked elaborately at the article referred to. ' I don't see any lady on the doormat,' he said.

' Here, listen, you—wise guy ! ' said Ivy in a considerable voice, ' don't you get fresh wi' me. I've got something to tell you that'll take the smile off of your face.'

' I'm not smiling.'

' Sez you ! That handle-bar moustache makes your face look like a bad accident to an onion.'

Peter fondled his tenderly reared moustache ; he had already suffered much in its cause in the workshops, but did not intend to endure banter from this unpleasant creature. ' Look here, Ivy,' he began, ' things are all up between you and me.'

' Oh, put a sock in the pi-jaw. Are ye comin' oot for a walk or are ye gonnae ask me into the hoose ? '

' I'm doing neither ! '

' Okay, well ! I'll jist stand here and yell at the top of my voice ! ' The volume of her vocal torrent increased as she added, ' I've went to the trouble of comin' up here——'

Peter shouted her down with : ' Nobody asked you to.'

' Is yer mother in ? '

' Why ? '

' Oh, I jist thought she'd be interested to hear about the mess her precious petsy-wetsy Peter's got mixed up in.'

' Me ? ' Peter's moustache lent emphasis to his query. ' Mixed up in a mess ? '

' Sure thing ! '

' You're cock-eyed, Ivy ! You've got nothing on me ! '

As was to be expected, the uproar filtered through to the kitchen, and Sarah, hearing it, bethought her of her neighbours' opinion of the McFlannel respectability. She hurried to the scene, saying :

' What's the matter ? You can't make that noise on the stairhead ! All the neighbours'll be listening. Come in, Ivy.'

' Suits me,' said the girl as she accepted the invitation.

' Let's go into the sitting-room,' pleaded Peter, but although his mother appreciated his anxiety for secrecy, she turned in the direction of the kitchen, saying that as his father and uncle were on the point of going out there was no need to burn unnecessary electricity.

' But Ivy wants a private talk with me alone ! ' protested Peter.

' Don't you worry yer wulkies about me. What I've came up for to say, youse can all hear.'

When they reached the kitchen it was to see that Willie and Mattha, far from going out, were settled comfortably in the two easy chairs. Sarah reminded her husband of his promise to show Mattha the correct way of pasting wallpaper.

'Ach, the morn's night'll dae,' procrastinated Willie. 'Mattha hasnae ony mair paste made up.'

Greetings and introductions being somewhat lukewarmly performed, Ivy was offered a chair by Sarah which she accepted and a cigarette by Mattha which she refused on the grounds, as she put it, that she preferred her clay pipe. Sarah regarded this statement as further evidence of the girl's deplorable background and retired to a corner to mourn her own ill-treatment.

'Is this the famous wireless set?' asked Ivy, nodding in the direction of a table model standing in the corner.

'What famous wireless set?' asked Maisie.

'The set Peter gi'en yez all fur yer Christmas last year.'

'What do *you* know about it?' Sarah emerged from her grief to inquire.

'That's what I've came up for to see Peter about,' declared Ivy.

'The wireless set!' gasped Sarah. 'Oh, what a relief! So it's not a . . . I mean—you don't want to marry Peter after all?'

'What! Me marry him? Not if ye were givin' him away with a quarter of tea! Forbye, jailbirds isn't in my line.'

'Jailbirds? You mean our Peter?' Sarah's emotions were on a see-saw.

'It's like this, well. I've jist new went to a job in a Sheriff Officer's. And this afternoon we got word to take out summonses for a hire-purchase firm. See?'

'I don't,' said Sarah. 'But go on.'

'Well, one of the summonses was for your Peter. For that wireless set!' Ivy pointed melodramatically, and the rest of the company gazed with renewed interest on the article they had long ago ceased to accept as anything but a noise-making machine. Maisie was the first to find her voice.

'Why? Was the wireless set not paid?'

'It was not!' Ivy was enjoying herself holding the centre of the stage. After giving Mattha a brief moment in which to exclaim, 'Imagine that !' she went on : 'But that's not what's botherin' me. He got my brother to sign as a guarantor, and I'm not goin' to let him get dragged in to a court case.'

'I don't get the hang of this at all !' stormed Peter. 'That wireless set was paid long ago.'

Sarah's 'Oh-dear-dear-this-is-terrible' was rather over-shadowed by a sudden movement on the part of Mattha who made for the door, saying that since his wife would be worrying about him he would be well advised to make for home quickly.

'You'll stay where you are !' Peter rounded on his uncle, seized him roughly by the arm and turned him to face the company again. 'It strikes me you're at the bottom of this !'

'Me ? Naw ! Whit should Ah ken aboot it ? See's me ma bunnet, Wullie.'

Peter struck down the outstretched hand before the bonnet could be placed in it. 'It was you that offered to get me the set, wasn't it ?'

'Ay. But Ah don't ken onythin' aboot it.' Finding his arms pinned as he strove to make a further attempt at egress, Mattha wailed, 'Aw, let me go, Peter. Ah wis jist sent oot fur a fish supper fur the wife. She'll gi'e me lalldy if Ah'm no' back.'

From behind, Peter's voice came thunderously : 'You said you could get me a wireless set cheap. You said you had lines for all the warehouses, didn't you ?'

'Ay, but heh, let me go, Peter. . . .'

While his father, mother and sister stood around in dumb-founderment, his ex-girl-friend exclaimed, 'Stick in till ye stick oot, Peter. Ye should of been a lawyer !'

Ignoring her, Peter swung the wretched Mattha round to face him, still keeping hold with one hand. 'Now, then, Uncle Matt—out with it ! You got me to take on that wireless set at five shillings a week, didn't you ?'

'Ay, but——' His protest ended on a yelp of pain. By accident or by design, Peter had moved so close to him that a few of his tender corns had been trampled on. He looked imploringly at his brother : 'Aw, heh, Wullie, can *you* no' let me oota here ? Ah'm needed at hame.'

'You'll get home when I'm done with you!' announced Peter.

'Oh, this is dreadful!' moaned Sarah. 'I'm fair ashamed, so I am! And me so proud of that nice wireless set.'

'After a month I was fed up with the bother of instalments, so I made up my mind I'd pay it in a lump sum. Isn't that right, Uncle Matt?'

'Ay, oh ay, but——'

'And I gave you the money?'

There being no negatived admission to that one, Willie exclaimed, 'Help ma boab, Mattha, don't say ye've embezzled it!'

'Naw—naw—Ah never. Ah——' Mattha suddenly found he had two jailers, one at each elbow.

'What have you done with the money, then? I gave you seventeen-pound-ten——'

'Ah—Ah cannae mind. Here, the wife'll gi'e me a bashin' if Ah don't hurry back wi' thae chips.'

'I feel like hurrying back with you and helping her to bash you,' said Sarah, her grief having given place to indignation; even Ivy was forgotten. 'This is just awful!'

Willie shook the elbow in his possession: 'Whit did ye dae wi' the money, Mattha?'

'Ah—Ah kep' up the instalments fur ages. As sure as daith Ah did, Peter. Ye don't need tae look at me like that.'

It was Peter's turn to shake an elbow: 'But you promised me you'd pay the whole lot at once!'

'Did you not get a receipt from him, Peter?' asked Maisie.

'No—I thought I could trust him.'

'Huh!' said Willie, tiring of his flabby burden and going towards a chair; 'trust oor Mattha?'

'Did you spend the money, Uncle Matt?' asked Maisie, who showed signs of taking over the cross-examination.

'Naw-naw!' Mattha seemed suddenly pleased to be telling the truth. 'Well, ye see, it wis like this—Ah wis—d'ye see, in the wey o' business of coorse . . .' He looked meaningly at Ivy.

'The sooner it's paid the better, well!' declared that young lady. 'I don't want my brother's name for to be dragged into the court.'

'Ah tell ye whit !' Abandoning his attempt at confession, Mattha was off once more on a business deal. 'Ah tell ye whit, Peter. Ye could sell yer set—Ah know somebody that wid buy it affa ye fur ten quid——'

'But I paid eighteen-ten !' protested Peter.

Mattha waved aside the interruption. 'An' look whit ye'd save on yer licence. They tell me the programmes isnae worth a quid a year.'

The thought of a house without a wireless set made Willie complain that he liked the wireless, but ! To which Peter pointed out that it was Uncle Matt's duty to pay up, not his.

'How much is still owing, Peter ?' asked Maisie.

'How should *I* know ? Do you, Ivy ?'

'Fourteen-pound-seventeen,' said the girl promptly.

'It's a lie !' snarled Mattha. 'Ah've peyed up faur mair nur that ! Ah'll get the pol—— the wife tae ye, so Ah will ! Ye're a wee twister, so ye are! Ah've a guid mind tae gi'e you a showin' up, so Ah have !'

'You give me a showin' up ! Huh, I like that !' retorted Ivy. 'You that's swindlin' yer own flesh an' blood !'

There was something overpowering in the way Mattha squared his shoulders and advanced omnipotently on the cowering Ivy. 'Swindlin',' he repeated. 'Don't talk tae me aboot swindlin' ! Ah'll tell them whit Ah done wi' that money ! Ah promised yer brother Ah widnae gi'e ye away, but Ah'm no' gonnae staun' here an' listen tae ony mair snash f'ae you !'

'You ain't got nothin' on me, big boy !' Her attempt at bluff was almost pitiful to the gaping audience.

'Oh, have Ah no' ? Well, listen tae this. Yer brother came tae me one day fur the len' o' fifteen quid. Ah tellt 'im Ah hadnae a' that money in the hoose, but he wis that desperate fur it that he offered me five shillin's in the pound interest.'

'Don't you say things like that aboot ma brother !' snapped Ivy.

'It's no' *him* Ah'm gettin' at ! Wait you ! Ah minded aboot this money o' Peter's, an' Ah wis awful sore needin' tae make some money on the side that Ah gi'en it tae yer brother—*an' 'e hasnae peyed me back !* '

Like a cornered cat, Ivy spat out, ' Ya dirty rat, ye ! I'll get the polis to ye for sayin' things like that about ma brother ! '

' Don't you call me a rat ! ' roared Mattha. ' D'ye know whit yer brother wanted the money fur ? Tae keep you f'ae goin' tae the nick ! Ye'd pinched money affa yer last boss ! '

With a darting movement, the convicted accuser got to the door before anyone could stop her, but she took time to deal Mattha a stinging blow on the face in the byegoing. As Mattha nursed the sore place and his brother stood poised in surprise, as Sarah plucked at her overworked neckband and Maisie folded her arms in an ' I-told-you-so ' attitude, Ivy slammed the outer door of the flat. Only Peter was relaxed enough to laugh. But there was more relief than merriment in his expression.

When the tension had eased, Sarah felt a sudden access of pity for her brother-in-law. She offered to bathe the stinging cheek and then, on being refused, offered to include Mattha in the tea-drinking ceremony she was about to prepare. This the man accepted, and for the next few minutes supplied further information as to the authenticity of his transactions with Ivy's brother. Willie was the first to offer a contribution towards the complete payment of the wireless set ; Maisie and Peter also naming their figure, Sarah could not but join in and, having signed a formal receipt for the whole sum, Mattha sat down with the rest of them round the table.

' Whit aboot yer wife's fish supper she sent ye fur, but ? ' asked Willie.

' Ach that ? ' Mattha dismissed the errand with a laugh. ' Ach, Ah jist sayed that.'

For once, Sarah had no criticism to offer on the question of her brother-in-law's morals.

CHAPTER 12

HOME IS THE SAILOR

ONE evening a few weeks later, Willie came home from his work to find Sarah on her knees ; the scrubbing brush in her hand precluded any suspicion that she was at her orisons. Nevertheless Willie was sufficiently surprised to demand :

' Whit the bleezes is goin' on here ? '

' I'm cleaning the house,' was the reply. ' Look '—she pointed with a dripping soapy brush—' a cable from Matt. He's coming home on leave.'

Without troubling to confirm her statement, Willie expressed his delight by asking when their son was to be expected.

' Next week.' Sarah went on scrubbing. ' Oh, I don't know whether I'm standing on my head or my heels.'

' But whit's the idea haein' a spring cleanin' a' ower again ? Ye had yin jist a month ago ! Ye surely don't expec' Matt tae go crawlin' aboot feelin' if there's dust ablow the pianna ? '

' Maybe not, but I want the satisfaction of knowing everything is spotless for him.'

Unable to see the finer points of her argument, Willie asked to see the cable ; when he had studied the form for a bit he complained that he would not have recognised Matt's handwriting. If the statement was intended to take his wife's mind off her present worries it failed in its purpose for she rose from her knees, emptied the pail of dirty water into the sink in the scullery and then ordered him to accompany her to the sitting-room as she wanted him to ' give her a hand.' For once he followed her meekly, only to find that he was expected to assist her in rolling up the carpet—a feat necessitating a great deal of manoeuvring of furniture. Peching ostentatiously, he kicked the resultant roll of Axminster and asked if he were expected to take it down to the back court and beat it.

'No-no. We don't need to do that now we've got a vacuum. Help me to carry it into the lobby.'

Willie seized one end of the unwieldy sausage and, piously proclaiming to Bonnie Scotland the extent of his sufferings in her cause, he wiggled himself backwards and in due course the carpet was dumped in the little lobby already jammed full of furniture from all parts of the house.

Dusting his hands, he said, ' Ye know, Serah, ye're makin' a mistake. Matt wid be the first tae say no' tae make a fuss ower the heid o' him comin' hame. He'll be that fed up wi' the wey things is kep' scrubbed on a ship, he'll be gled tae come hame tae a wee bit dirt ! '

' Are you trying to make out that I keep a dirty house ? '

' It must be durty or ye wouldnae be wantin' tae clean it ! '

Sarah's temper was not under full control. She almost shrieked the retort, ' I only want to keep it from getting dirty ! It's a shame, so it is, you telling me I keep a dirty house and me working my fingers to the bone. I get no thanks for all I do. I'm just a slave in this house.'

' Aw heh, Serah, don't screw on the watter-works. Ah only said that Matt bein' on a ship wid be fed up wi' polishin' brasses an' scrubbin' floors——'

But once again he had said the wrong thing for Sarah snapped back, ' Who's asking him to polish brasses and scrub floors at home ? '

' No' me ! '

' You did so ! Not content with telling me I keep a dirty house you're trying to make out now I would ask Matt to scrub and polish for me.'

' Ach ! ' said the man in exasperation ; ' ye're bawlin' doon the wrang lum. Ah never said . . .' He broke off feeling the futility of self-justification with Sarah in this mood. ' Whit d'ye want me tae dae noo ? Whitewash a ceilin' ? '

' That's right—change the subject ! ' Sarah sniffed. ' Here's me toiling and moiling from morning till night and nobody ever thinks of giving me a word of appreciation ! '

' If it comes tae that, naebody ever gi'es me a word o' appreciation eithers. D'ye think the manager comes tae me an' slaps me on the back an' says, " Jolly good show, McFlannel ! Those rivets are——" '

His impersonation act was rudely interrupted. ' Don't make a fool of me ! And anyway, you get paid for what you do ! '

' Ah-ha ! ' Willie thought he had found the root of the matter. ' So that's it ! You've been readin' *The Daily Bugle* aboot wages fur wives or somethin'.'

' I have not ! I've no time for reading. When I'm done with the housework I've got to start darning and mending——'

' Well, if ye're as hashed as a' that, whit are ye wastin' time cleanin' the hoose fur Matt comin' hame ? '

' Because I want everything to be spotless for him.'

' Ach, this is whaur we came in ! ' Willie was turning away in disgust when he remembered he was expected to act as a house-wife's assistant. ' Whit else d'ye want tae dae ? '

While Sarah was still thinking up how best to employ such willing labour the outer door opened and Peter stepped into their midst. He gaped at the cluttered lobby and exclaimed :

' Help—what's this in aid of ? '

Said Willie with some feeling : ' Matt's comin' hame tae eat 'is meals aff the floor.'

Peter seized on the first three words of the explanation. ' Boy, that's great ! ' he enthused. ' Is he bringing you a parrot, Dad ? '

Willie admitted that the possibility had not yet occurred to him but agreed that a parrot in the house would be a fair divert.

' When's he arriving, Mother ? ' asked Peter, and the reply ' Next week ' was so sulky that he went on, ' I say—what's the matter ? Are you not well, Mother ? '

Willie answered for her, ' She's in the huff because we don't come hame every night screamin' aboot whitna swell job she's made o' dustin' the pawrlur.'

Peter goggled his bewilderment but made no comment on this

revelation of his lack of appreciation of his mother's artistry. He allowed himself to be brushed aside to make room for a further chair which Sarah silently, but with a great deal of emphasis, laid down. To relieve the tension he asked where Maisie was, but the only reply he got was a cross ' I don't know,' so he said :

' Oh, come off it, Mother. I thought you'd 've been up to ninety-nine with delight at the thought of Matt coming home.'

' So I was—until your father started casting up to me that I kept a dirty house.'

' Ah never said nae sich thing ! ' came the protest from a safe corner.

' You did so ! '

' Well, Ah only said it fur yer ain good. Ye'll loss a' yer guid looks if ye keep on cairryin' on the wey ye're daein'. Ye don't want Matt tae ask if ye've been ill ? '

' That's right,' said Peter, entering into the spirit of the thing. ' Come on—we'll help you to clean up the house ! '

' The house isn't dirty ! ' Sarah almost yelled the statement.

'Ach, gi'e it up, son,' said Willie. ' She's got ye every wey ! '

The three of them were glowering at one another when once again the door opened and Maisie came into the rather prickly bosom of her family.

' Hallo—what have we here ? ' she demanded. ' A delayed-action bomb ? '

' Now don't *you* start ! ' snapped her mother.

' Matt's coming home next week,' said Peter, attempting to explain.

' Oh goody ! Mother—we'll need to have everything absolutely shining for him ! '

Sarah's tears could no longer be sniffed back. ' Oh, Maisie,' she bubbled, ' you're the only one who's got any sense in this house ! ' Seeing the bewilderment in the girl's face, she went on, ' I've had a terrible time with these two—telling me I keep a dirty house and making a fool of me because I want a little appreciation and——'

Maisie led her mother towards the kitchen. ' You're tired,

that's what it is,' she said sympathetically. 'See—I'll help you. What'll I do first?'

'Whit aboot takin' the coal oota the bunker an' washin' it?' suggested her father, nudging Peter who added gigglingly:

'Or what about whitewashing the inside of the kitchen chimney?'

'They're just teasing you, Mother,' whispered Maisie, at which Sarah managed to make a final and effective sniff, banishing her tears and revealing a courageous smile.

A week later, the last brass knob having been polished, the last carpet swept, the last cushion shaken, Sarah, Willie and Peter assembled themselves in the kitchen before going to the station to meet the returning sailor. Sarah peered at herself in the scrap of mirror above the sewing-machine and declared she didn't know whether she liked her new hat or not.

'It looks like a pea on the tap o' a drum,' said Willie.

'Dad!' protested Maisie; 'must you always say the nastiest thing you can think of, or are you just trying to hide your feelings?'

'Ah'm jist thinkin',' he went on unheeding, 'Matt'll no' likely know ye in yer fur coat, Serah. Ye're like the en' o' a hoose in it.'

'Oh, Willie,' said Sarah, 'it was you that gave me the fur coat. I put it on because if any of the other officers are along with him I don't want him to be ashamed of his mother.'

'In that case, Peter, you an' me wid be better tae pit on wur lum hats!'

Peter agreed. 'We'd look like station masters,' he said.

'Ay—or cabbies.'

Without giving them time to allow their imagination to run riot, Sarah hustled them towards the door, reminding Maisie to see that the halibut was ready to put in the pan as soon as the party returned.

Willie, catching the word halibut, complained, 'Ye're no' gi'ein' Matt fish fur 'is tea, are ye? Help ma boab, he'll want tae forget a' aboot the sea. Could ye no'a gi'en 'im ham an' eggs?'

'What would we have used for eggs, Dad?' asked Maisie sweetly.

Unable to think of an answer, Willie followed his wife and son out of the house. As was to be expected with a marshalling force like Sarah, the party arrived at the station fifteen minutes too soon, to find that the train would be fifty minutes late; the result being that when it finally steamed into the station Sarah was rather mottled of countenance with excitement. Conscious of the fact, she sought comfort from her husband. 'Do I look as awful as I feel?' she asked.

Candidly he replied, after a searching look, 'Ay, ye're gey bad lookin', but, ach! a man rinnin' fur 'is life wid never notice onythin'.' He turned his attention to his son: 'Peter—away you an' staun' at the other barrier an' gi'e us a whistle if Matt comes oot your wey.'

Peter fingered his facial new-fanglement. 'Maybe Matt won't know me with my moustache!' he said.

'That's no' a moustache, it's a soup strainer!' commented Willie.

Peter was starting out on some sort of statement which was intended to point out that he had to restore the balance of nature, since his father had decided a few months previously to shave off his thirty-year-old Charlie Chaplin model, but Sarah would have none of it. Peter went off hopefully to the other barrier.

True to form, Sarah's mind dwelt on lots of things calculated to worry her. 'It's an awful busy train,' she observed. 'I hope we don't miss him. The light's awful poor.'

'Hoo could we miss 'im an' three o' us lookin' fur 'im—an' him lookin' fur us forbye!' Suddenly he started yelling, 'Matt! Matt! Here we are!'

'Don't bawl like that!' said Sarah shamefacedly. 'That's not Matt!'

'Neither it is,' admitted Willie. 'Ah jist seen a sailor an' thocht it wis sure tae be oor Matt.'

'You seem to forget that he's an officer now. He'll not be dressed like that.'

'That's right. Ah'll need tae mind an' say "sir" tae'm noo!'

Wishing she had stayed at home and so saved her complexion from this burning excitement, Sarah stood on tiptoe at the back of the crowd and, spying a white cap in the distance, asked if this was Matt now.

'Naw, it's no' Matt,' said Willie, having a better view on account of his six extra inches ; 'that's an auld man wi' a beard. Jeengs, his wife'll be able tae stuff a coupla pillows the day he shaves that off.'

But Sarah was not interested in pillow stuffing. 'D'you not see any more white caps ? '

'Naw—if you werenae sae fat Ah'd gi'e ye a leg-up so's ye could look ower the folks' heids. Jeengs, Serah, ye're twice the size ye were the last time Matt wis hame.'

'Oh, be quiet, you ! People'll hear you. . . . Goodness, d'you not see him yet ? '

'Naw—you should be able tae see 'im better nor me—noo that ye've stertit wearin' specs ! '

Right enough, thought Sarah, they had all of them changed quite a bit since Matt was home last, but then a new worry assailed her. What if he had missed the train—or, better still from a worrying point of view—what if he had met with an accident ? 'Oh dear, I'm frightened, Willie,' she said aloud.

'How—whit's up ? Are ye gettin' suffocated wi' the crush ? '

'No—I'm sure something's wrong. Matt would've been first out of the carriage. You know what he is. Oh dear-dear, this is terrible.'

'Here ! ' exclaimed Willie ; 'did ye see that auld sailor chap wi' the beard when 'e passed us the noo ? Did ye see whitna hard look he gi'en us ? '

'Oh, never mind old sailors with beards. I want to see Matt ! '

Meanwhile, at home, Maisie was putting the finishing touches to the tea-table that was set with such lavish abundance in honour of the sailor son's homecoming. Extravagantly, because it was such a special occasion, she was dipping the halibut steaks in beaten egg when the doorbell rang. Washing her hands, she hurried to the door wondering why her father had not used his doorkey as was his wont. On the doormat stood a tall figure, his face well hidden behind a luxuriant growth of hair ; his white cap gleamed at her in the mirk of the stairhead.

'Hallo, Maisie,' came a familiar voice from the depths of the full stand of whiskers ; 'don't you know me ? '

'It's not . . . Matt ! Oh, Matt ! ' They were in each other's arms in a flash. 'Matt—I can't believe it's you after all those years ! '

'Get on with you—it's only ten months since I was home last.'

'No wonder I didn't know you with that disguise on your face.' She hugged him again and then demanded, 'I say— where's everybody else ? '

'No idea. Did a search-party go out to meet me ? '

'Sure thing. Mother all dolled up in her fur coat, and Dad wearing a hat for a change. Peter too ! '

The sailor did not view the situation with as much dismay as his sister ; he began to lug indoors some of the baggage that was sprayed about him on the landing. Maisie, however, could not let the mystery go unprobed.

'Are you sure you didn't see any of them at the station ? '

'Absolutely positive ! I had a good look round, and then I saw I was going to miss the chance of a taxi so I came on, thinking maybe you hadn't got the wire I'd sent off from Liverpool this morning.'

'Oh, we got it all right. Mother's been in such a stew since your cable arrived last week. I wonder if they went to the wrong station ? '

'Which did they go to ? '

'Central.'

'That's where I came in all right.'

'I can quite imagine Dad missing you, but not Mother *and* Peter. I hope there's nothing wrong.'

'D'you think I ought to go and look for them ? '

'Oh, give them a wee while. Come on—I'll help you to stow your luggage into your room.'

'Still the same old cabin?'

'Sure. Walk this way, please.'

With typical Scots reticence, Matt tried to extract some confidences while they were walking towards the bedroom in single file and no longer facing each other. 'How are the boy friends these days, Maisie?'

'Oh, pretty much about the same.'

'Nobody special yet?'

'I don't think so. What about yourself? Got a wife in every port?'

'Not so far as I know.' He could be as off-hand as she when it came to withholding information. 'Listen! I think I hear voices on the stair!'

Maisie listened. 'It's them! I tell you what, Matt—let's have some fun! You kid on you're somebody else! Hurry! Get those bags out of sight and then you scoot into the sitting-room. Quick. Keep in the shadow!'

The scuffle was over before the door had opened, and by the time the three disappointed members of the family had filed into the lobby Maisie was there too, putting on an act of expectancy and amazement.

'What's wrong?' she managed to say. 'Is Matt not with you?'

'Is he not here?' countered Sarah embarrassingly.

Before Maisie had time to think out an evasive answer, her father got in with: 'He musta missed the train. Ah've been sayin' that a' the road hame.'

Sarah's sharp eyes saw the light in the sitting-room and demanded to know the reason for it. 'Don't say we've got a visitor—tonight of all nights!'

'It's a fellow from the same boat as Matt,' said Maisie. 'He dropped in to see us.'

Saying, 'How is it that he got here and Matt didn't?' Sarah strode into the sitting-room neck and neck with Willie who, on seeing the shadow-dimmed figure, exclaimed:

'Jeengs—it's the auld sailor chap Ah seen at the station! Hoo'ye?'

In a disguised voice Matt said ' How d'you do,' and extended his hand.

Maisie said, ' This is Mother—you've maybe heard Matt speak about her.'

Once again the visitor held out his hand, saying ' How d'you do ' in a sepulchral voice.

' How d'you do,' said Sarah, adding : ' There's something familiar about you.'

' And this,' went on Maisie, pushing Peter in front of the sailor, ' behind the handle-bar moustache, is Brother Peter.'

Somewhat self-consciously Peter acknowledged the introduction, while his mother bent a bewildered gaze on the stranger.

' Why was Matt not on that train ? ' she asked.

Seeing her pathetic concern and being himself overcome with emotion, Matt could contain himself no longer. With outstretched hands he came out of the shadows, saying in his own voice that was somehow unfamiliar :

' Oh, Mother, don't you know me ? '

' Matt ! Oh, Matt ! ' Sarah fell into the waiting arms, buried her face between the beard and the black tie and allowed her tears of joy to spill on the immaculate white collar.

' Help ma boab,' said Willie, ' it's Matt himsel'.' He gripped a hand that was doing its best to comfort a sobbing woman.

Peter gripped the other hand. ' Matt ! I saw you at the station. You looked at me ! Did you not recognise me ? '

' How could I ? And you hiding behind that moustache ? '

' Listen tae him talkin' ! ' jeered Willie. ' An' him wi' a beard like a shovel ! ' He blew his nose noisily. ' Did ye no' see us at the station ? '

' I did—but I never thought for a moment it was you ! Mother looks so opulent in her new fur coat and that ridiculous little hat—and the spectacles too ! '

' Ah tellt ye it wis a daft-like hat, Serah ! '

The jibe had no power to wound her at this shining moment ; nevertheless she lifted her begrutten face and said, ' Oh, Matt— am I terribly changed ? '

' Well . . .' Matt searched for words that would be tactful.

'Come on—oot wi't!' said his father. 'She's pittin' on weight!'

'Well—let's say there's all the more of her to love—eh, Mother?'

'Oh, Matt, you say the nicest things!'

'D'ye see ony difference on me?' asked Willie.

'Of course! I would never have known you in that hat—and besides, with your moustache off——'

Maisie interposed with: 'But why the face-fungus on your own dial, Matt? You're not hiding from justice, are you?'

'No-no,' he laughed. 'I just thought I'd give you a surprise. I'm shaving it off tomorrow.'

'Whit did Ah tell ye, Serah? There's anuff hair there tae stuff a mattress.'

Sarah roused herself from her happy weeping. 'Here—what are we all standing here blethering for? Maisie—is the halibut ready?'

'My goodness! I forgot all about it!' She hurried off to the scullery, with her mother close on her heels shedding fur coat and new hat recklessly at the hallstand. Willie joined them in the kitchen.

'Ah don't see nae signs o' that parrot, Serah. Ah hope he hasnae brung yin, fur some o' them's kinna vulgar, ye know.'

'D'you think there's any chance of nylons for me, Mother?' shouted Maisie from the scullery.

'I'd rather have some tins of fruit,' replied the housewife.

In a few minutes Matt was with them lugging his largest suit-case which he spread open on the sewing-machine. To keep the smell of frying fish from spreading through the flat, Maisie shut the scullery door, whispering to her mother, 'If you hear the love-call of a nylon, let me know.' Matt must have heard for he lifted a parcel from his case, went to the scullery door and, opening it, pushed the parcel through the aperture, saying, 'Here you are—three pairs, fully fashioned!'

Cooking knife in hand, Maisie threw herself into her brother's arms and took up much the same position as her mother had done a few minutes previously. Her kisses were so plentiful that Matt had to protest he didn't want to have to comb her out of his beard.

'Oh, I can hardly believe it—three whole pairs of nylons ! The only decent pair of stockings I've got are lisle drain-pipes. Oh, thanks a million, Matt.'

She turned to the smoking fat in the frying pan and Matt left her, shutting the scullery door after him. From the case he took another parcel—this time for his mother—and since it contained a large quantity of tinned fruit she was suitably grateful. For Peter there were some cigars designated 'squibs' by Matt, and for his father, who was trying to look disinterested and not succeeding too well, there was also a small parcel which Matt said frankly was 'a book.'

'A bub-book !' stammered Willie, making no attempt to accept the gift. 'Thuth-that's real kind o' ye, Matt, but Ah'm no' much o' a reader, ye know.'

'What's it called ?' Peter opened the parcel, looked at the title on the spine of the book. 'Sweet Moments by S. U. Gar-Cane,' he read. 'Can't say I've ever heard of the author. It sounds like poetry. Dad writes his own poetry nowadays, you know, Matt !'

'Is that a fact ? Are you not going to have a look at your book, Dad ?'

'Ach, it'll dae the morn. Ma eyes is kinna tired the night. Heh, Serah, hoo's the halibut gettin' on ?'

'Maisie's getting it ready,' answered Sarah, putting some more cakes on the table. 'Matt, that was awful nice of you to give your father a book. It'll be something for him to read in the winter.'

Willie scratched his head uncomfortably. 'Jeengs, the last book Ah read wis Deadwood Dick,' he said not quite truthfully. 'Ah'm feart Sweet Moments isnae much in ma line, Matt.'

'All the same, Dad, I think you ought to have a look at it.'

'So Ah will,' he promised ; then, suddenly realising that a change of subject was the best way out of the difficulty, he strode over to the scullery door, saying, 'Here—whit's Maisie thinkin' aboot—that halibut's had time tae walk tae the table an' back.

Ah'll need tae see whit's keepin' her.' Paying no attention to his wife's injunction to be patient and to look at his book, he went into the scullery. There he found Maisie sniffing suspiciously. He shut the door.

'Whit's up?' he demanded.

'Whsh, Dad.'

In a hoarse whisper that could be heard above the splutter of frying fish he repeated his query : 'Whit are ye greetin' fur?'

'I'm not greeting,' she sniffed.

'Come on, lass—tell yer auld faither,' he went on tenderly.

'It's the stockings, Dad. They're no use to me.'

'Whit wey? Are they too wee?'

'No—too big. I take size eight-and-a-half and they're size ten.' She wiped her eyes with a corner of her overall.

'Could ye no' pit a tuck in the toe, well?'

'Don't be silly, Dad. They're too wide in the legs too. Oh, it's a shame, and I was so desperately needing them !'

'Pit a tuck up the backs o' the legs, well. It wid never be seen !'

'Oh, forget it, Dad. Whatever you do, don't let on to Matt. I'm not wanting to hurt his feelings.'

At that the door opened and Matt appeared through the steam with another parcel in his hand. 'I say, Maisie,' he said rather self-consciously, 'I've made a mistake. I've given you the wrong parcel. Here's yours. Eight-and-a-half's your size, isn't it?'

Once again the fish was forgotten as Maisie dealt with her emotions ; when Matt was smoothing out his beard after the onslaught of Maisie's gratitude, Willie asked :

'An' who wis the size tens meant fur, Matt?'

'Ah-ha—you would like to know—eh? They're for a *great* friend, Dad !' said Matt.

'Great's the word,' said Willie, laughing at his own joke ; 'great big feet. Here—are ye sure ye widnae like tae gi'e 'er *Sweet Moments* or whitever ye ca' it? It wid be mair in hur line.'

'Why? Have you got an eye on her nylons? No, Dad, *Sweet Moments* is all yours. Do have a look inside.'

'Have ye written somethin' on the first page?'

'Look and see.'

Since there seemed no help for it, Willie lifted the book again and tried to open it in the normal way ; baffled, he examined it fore and aft, finally discovering that it was not a book really but a box of chocolates made up to look like one. His delight was unbounded and, hearing the rustle of paper, Susan crept from her basket by the fireside and sat at his feet until the inevitable portion came to her from Willie's mouth. Sarah was naturally annoyed by this blunting of the edge of her husband's appetite, but she need not have worried ; the appetite in question was not so easily blunted. When the fish had been eaten and they were still at the scone-and-tea-bread course, Willie said :

'Heh, Matt—Ah meant tae ask ye. Did ye notice an' awful difference in the hoose f'ae the last time ye were hame ? '

Matt looked round inquiringly before admitting that the place looked the same as usual to him.

'Is it no' a lot cleaner ? ' persisted his father.

'No. I can't say it is. I don't see the slightest difference.'

Turning to his wife, Willie exclaimed, ' Whit did Ah tell ye, Serah ? Ye've had a' yer work fur nothin' ! It's *you* he wants tae see when he comes hame—no' the hoose ! ' He paused while mother and son exchanged an affectionate look. ' Just,' he added with an attempt at off-handedness, '. . . just like the rest o' us ! '

PRINTED IN GREAT BRITAIN AT
THE PRESS OF THE PUBLISHERS